The Witch and the Jaguar

TERRY SPEAR

PUBLISHED BY:

Terry Spear

The Witch and the Jaguar

Copyright © 2018 by Terry Spear

Discover more about Terry Spear at:

http://www.terryspear.com/

ISBN-13: 978-1-63311-040-3

DEDICATION

To Demetra Toula Iliopoulos for loving my books no matter the season! Thanks for being a fan!

ACKNOWLEDGMENTS

Thanks so much to Darla Taylor and Donna Fournier for beta reading for me and helping to make the story the best, even during the Thanksgiving holidays!

CHAPTER 1

Jaguar shifter Erin Hawkins was glad that she didn't have a mission as a JAG agent—a special jaguar shifter policing force that she worked for—over Halloween, one of her favorite days of the year and she hoped she didn't get called up for anything. She'd worked the last three years during All Hallows Eve: the first case—saving a jaguar family being hunted in the Amazon one year, helping to find a jaguar's family after he'd lost them in the jungle the next year, and searching for jaguar poachers that she had to eliminate the year after that.

This year, she was all set. After returning home from the last two weeklong mission yesterday, she had two weeks off from the job to recuperate.

Before she headed over to the jaguar party, she tried to deposit a check a friend gave her to pay for her own witch's costume when she'd forgotten her wallet at home, but the online bank app couldn't read the routing number no matter how many times Erin retook a picture of it and tried to deposit it. Okay, so it *was* Halloween. If anything weird was going to happen, this should be the day for it.

Her hair dyed purple, she had already dressed in her purple and black witch costume: a black corset, long, black gloves, a longer overskirt open in the front to reveal a short, purple skirt trimmed in black lace, black fishnet stockings, and black high-heeled boots. She wanted to arrive early at the party to see if the hosts needed any additional assistance with setting up anything else at their house. Her brother was off working for the JAG this Halloween, so she knew he wouldn't be there, being his overly protective, brotherly self. The thing of it was, she'd saved his butt as many times as he'd saved hers on missions. She really didn't need his protection at a shifter party!

She thought his overprotectiveness was a ploy to garner single she-cats' attentions.

She had time before her friend was picking her up, and she decided to run over to the bank that was located only a half mile away, then drop by the grocery store and pick up some Halloween cupcakes.

She planned to just go through the drive-thru to deposit the check, but every line had four cars stacked up, and there was only one car parked out front. Exasperated, she parked her car, grabbed her hat—no decently-dressed witch would ever go out in public without it—put it on her head, and walked inside the small bank. Sure enough, there was only one male customer at the counter, and the other teller was free.

Erin hurried up to the counter, and the bank clerk smiled. "I love your costume and your hair to match."

Erin smiled. "Thanks. It's totally a new look for me." Not that she didn't love to have fun and do something daring and different.

Of course, the first time she shifted, the purple hair dye would be gone, but she didn't plan to turn into her jaguar anytime soon. She filled out the deposit slip, then handed the slip and the check to the teller.

A male customer entered the bank and stood right behind Erin, way too close. He was practically breathing down her neck, annoying her. He was supposed to stand behind the velvet rope until the next available teller was ready for him. Erin took her receipt, thanked the teller, and turned to leave, wanting to glower or growl at the annoying man, but she curbed the inclination. Cold blue eyes stared at her for a moment—maybe he didn't like witches—and she smiled at him, figuring that might change his grouchy expression. It didn't. And that's when she realized he had his hand tucked inside his black hoody, as though he was a Napoleon wannabe. A hand on a gun? A bank robber?

She moved out of his way, hoping she was just being paranoid. In her line of work, she was wary of situations that could be bad news. She would call the police once she was outside, if she believed there was more to this, like a getaway car parked right outside, engine running, and a nervous-looking dude driving it.

Before she could leave the bank, a tall, dark-haired man dressed as a musketeer, plumed hat, cape, and sword included, walked inside and smiled at her, as if he

3

appreciated that she was dressed in costume also. At once, she smelled he was a jaguar. Her job was to protect jaguars, though she was also on-hand to help humans too. But she wanted to ensure she wasn't just calling in a false alarm.

She glanced around the bank, two loan officers, the two bank tellers, hoody guy, and the musketeer. Now she was torn about what to do. She was trained to take down suspects, but she wasn't a cop with the local police force. She was part of a jaguar policing force that had badges, making them appear to be a special unit of the FBI. Since humans didn't know the shifters existed, that's how they policed their own kind.

"Hey, don't I know you?" she asked, hoping to get the musketeer to agree to go with her for a cup of coffee or something to get him out of the building, just in case a bank robbery was in progress.

He smiled at her again, as if he thought she was giving him a come-on line. She loved his radiant smile, as though she had just made his day. Before he could answer her, another man walked into the bank and blocked the doors, wearing the same kind of black hoodie, except he was wearing a black ski mask and she knew then a bank robbery was going down.

"Bank robbery is in progress, guy behind you and the guy behind me are involved, I think," she quickly warned the musketeer, her voice low for his hearing only.

"I'm an off-duty cop, Bryce Jenkins. Leave if you can and call the police."

"Everyone, get down on the ground!" the armed robber at the door ordered. That was their cue that they weren't leaving to warn anybody about anything.

The one with the teller ordered her to fill up a couple of black bags he had hidden under his hoody.

Bryce and Erin quickly got down on the floor next to each other while the loan officers were made to lie down on the floor also.

"What the hell," the robber near the glass doors said as a car sped past the bank.

The getaway driver?

"You, witch, get up. You're coming with us," the robber said.

She figured he planned to use *her* car as a getaway. She wasn't about to be taken hostage. She figured they'd just take her car and kill her and dump her body somewhere else. When she didn't move, the guy came after her and grabbed her arm. Bryce started to move to free her, but she pretended to go along with the plan, rising to her feet in her high-heeled boots, twisted her arm free from the robber's meaty grip, and kneed him hard in the groin. When he bent over in pain, she jerked her knee up to hit him in the chin, knocking him back.

She realized then the man with the money bags was coming at them, gun out while she was taking the other man down with a swift kick of her leg. Bryce was already on his feet, swinging his musketeer sword at the other bank robber, knocking the gun out of his hand.

Patrol cars were pulling up outside. One of the bank staff must have hit a silent alarm.

Using handcuffs, Bryce secured the man's hands behind him.

"Do you always carry handcuffs with you?" she asked, tying up the other guy's wrists with a plastic tie.

Bryce smiled at her. "Do you always carry plastic ties with you?" He pulled out his cell phone and called to the police outside that the two bank robbers were in custody and the getaway driver had torn off. He gave them a description of the driver's vehicle as six police officers stormed into the bank.

After they gave their statements and the men were hauled off, Bryce asked, "Hey, you want a cup of coffee after I make a withdrawal?"

"I've got to run, but yeah. Some other time would be great." She pulled out her JAG agent card and handed it to him, not wanting him to believe she was just saying that and really didn't want to get together with him. She really did want to go out with him. At least once. Any guy who could tackle a gunman with a sword made her want to learn more about him.

The adrenalin still rushing through her blood, she hurried out of the bank and headed over to the grocery store. She realized there wasn't a soul parked at the drive-thru now. They must have gotten word there was a robbery in progress.

Not the best way to start out her nice quiet vacation from work, but it could have been worse.

***

"Hell," Bryce's police partner, wolf shifter Jack Wolff, said to him as they wrapped up the business with the bank robbers. "First you and a, uh, one of your kind get the drop on two bank robbers, and then she turns you down for a date? Coffee? You should have offered her a meal, wine, dancing, something more, at the very least."

"She probably had a party to go to." Bryce was certain she'd take him up on his next offer when she was available. He couldn't believe the woman he had seen in JAG training that he was interested in dating had helped him thwart a bank robbery. The purple hair had thrown him off though and he hadn't recognized her.

"I can't believe you used a sword on the guy, and the little lady only employed martial arts. Seems like a match made in heaven. Unless she cast a witch's spell on the poor bastard."

"She's a JAG agent," Bryce said for Jack's ears only as they headed out of the bank.

"No, kidding?" Jack smiled. "Now I wish a woman like that came in wolf form."

Bryce chuckled. "Someday you'll get lucky. Not that this means this will go anywhere between us either. Are you still going to a party?"

"Yeah, but unlike you, I'll go like I am. The ladies love a guy in uniform."

"They don't know you're all wolf. I've got to run and grab something at the grocery store."

"Hell of a way to spend your off-duty time."

"Yeah, I was just doing my civic duty." And helping the she-cat stop the robbery. How would it have looked to his fellow officers if she had done all the work?

"See you Monday then."

"See you then." Bryce was hopeful that the JAG agent was going to the same party he was going to tonight. If so, he wanted to dance with her, as long as she wasn't already seeing someone else. He smiled. He was still going to ask her to dance, if she was there. When did he *not* live dangerously?

CHAPTER 2

As soon as Erin arrived home, her best friend Bethany called. "Hey, are you ready?"

"Absolutely."

Erin could tell Bethany was on her Bluetooth and on her way over to pick her up at the home where she and her brother lived.

"Witch's costume is in perfect order, hair a bright, pretty red—I can't believe you turned yours purple—and I'm all set to go. Thanks bunches for putting my costume on your credit card when I forgot my wallet at home."

"No problem at all. I've had my credit card sitting on my desk to place an online order and left it at home accidentally. I know how annoying it can be." Erin set the container of cupcakes on the table near the door along with her hat so she wouldn't forget anything. "I couldn't get the bank app to recognize it though."

"Oh, that sucks."

"Yeah, so I dropped by the bank to deposit it."

"Don't tell me you had trouble depositing it there."

"Nope. There was a bank robbery in progress." Erin knew her best friend would have wanted to be there to help her out. Erin was glad she hadn't been in harm's way also.

"Ohmigod, are you okay?"

"Yeah." Erin explained everything that went on.

"Wait, back up to the cute jaguar musketeer. Why didn't you invite him to the party?"

"I'm not hosting it and he's not on our shifter force."

"Family and friends are invited! Do you have his number? *I'll* invite him!"

Erin laughed. "No. He was going to his own party, from the looks of the way he was dressed."

Bethany gave an exaggerated sigh. "It seems unreal that you and I are both off from the JAG branch for All Hallows Eve this year. It's been forever since we've been able to do this together."

"Three's a charm. Hopefully, we won't get called to take care of a job while we're there. We have a full moon out, you know. A full moon always seems to bring out the crazies, more so than usual." Erin had been so happy that both of them were off from work so they could dress as sister witches this year. They loved to wear different but matching costumes. They'd been like sisters growing up and had even gone to the same jaguar daycare run by one of the agent's mothers. They were shocked to learn wolf shifters existed and that now the jaguar daycare was taking in wolves. She thought that could be fun for the little ones.

"And James isn't going to be there either? I heard he had an assignment in Belize, chasing down more jaguar poachers. It's like a deadly game of whack-a-mole."

"Right. I agree. But it's a good thing for me that he's not going to be at the party."

"*I'm* disappointed," Bethany said. "I'd hoped to see your SEAL brother. Hot stuff."

"He doesn't ever go to the parties, except when he was dating Jane that one year, and unless I'm going to be there."

"As a chaperone, I know," Bethany said and laughed. "I still can't believe he took her to the Halloween party and then she dumped him. And on top of that, that she'd been with the guy she threw him over for. You know, she's going to be there this year too."

"Yeah, if I had real witch's powers to deal with her, I'd turn her into a toad." Though Erin had suspected that's where James and Jane's relationship had been going because of the number of times he tried to set up a date with her and she'd turned him down for one reason or another. If she had really wanted to go out with him, Jane would have made some time for him. Jane was a JAG agent like them, and Erin had really liked her, until she dumped her brother. Erin was glad she hadn't been paired up to work with her on assignments of late because of that. Though Erin was a professional, and she would have put aside her misgivings had she had to work with her.

"You and me both. I'll be there in about twenty minutes."

"All right. See you then." Erin slipped her phone into her pocket when someone pounded on the door. *Trick-or-*

treaters. She picked up her black witch's cauldron off the kitchen counter, filled with fun-size packages of candy, and headed for the door. Before she answered it, she grabbed her hat and stuck it on her head. When she opened the door, she was expecting to see little kids all dressed in costumes.

Instead, her brother was standing there, bags in hand, handsome, muscled, a she-cat's dream, if he ever chose to settle down. Bethany was one of his biggest admirers, but even she couldn't get his attention.

Erin closed her gaping mouth. "What are you doing here?" As if her brother didn't live here! Erin hadn't meant to sound so annoyed, but she really didn't want her brother's overprotectiveness tonight. She was a JAG agent too and very capable of dealing with whatever he was worried she'd have difficulty with. "You lost your key again."

"Temporarily misplaced." He smiled and looked in her cauldron of candy. "The good stuff. All chocolate. Set some aside for me, will you? This is a new look for you. Purple hair?" He entered the house and carried his bags to his bedroom.

She shut the door and set the cauldron of candy on the table. "First jaguar shift and it will be gone." She was glad she had the time off from her work for a couple of weeks because purple hair wasn't regulation. They could wear just about anything they wanted clothes-wise, as long as it helped them to get the job done, but purple hair just was a little too showy. "I'm going to a Halloween party." She hated to tell him, but he wasn't leaving and he'd know she was going— and not because she was just dressed up to hand out candy— as soon as Bethany arrived.

She knew her brother didn't like Halloween parties, not after his former girlfriend dumped him in a big row at last year's party. Bethany had told her all about it. Her brother had never spoken about it to her otherwise. Jane had broken up with James, all because she'd met some other jaguar. He wasn't part of their special, jaguar policing force, but was a real cop on the human police force.

Which was all right with them, because any of the jaguars who could work secretly among the humans and help other jaguars out was a good thing. But it also meant no one would hassle him for fear they'd get ticketed. Though Erin had heard the man—she didn't know his name—was soon going to be a homicide detective.

"You're not going without me," James said.

She let out her breath in exasperation. "You have to wear a costume."

He dropped his bags in his bedroom.

She followed him into the room. "You can't go unless you're dressed in a costume." She was certain he didn't have anything lying around to wear for the party. But she knew that stubborn look he was wearing meant he was going no matter what. "What if Jane is there?"

He grunted.

She smiled. Then she frowned. She hoped he didn't think he might get back together with her. Since Jane was going with another jaguar now, Erin thought that she liked that he wasn't with the JAG branch.

"Why do you think you have to be so overprotective of me when I'm just going to a party? I'm a JAG agent just like you, for heaven's sake," she said.

The doorbell rang and he pulled off his shirt. She huffed and headed for the front door. When she answered it, she was expecting Bethany, but a bunch of trick-or-treaters held up their sacks for treats. She passed out candy to the passel of Star Wars outfitted kids—one Darth Vader and two storm troopers. Then she had an idea. James could just stay here and hand out candy to the kids. Like that would go over big with him. The kids thanked her and ran to the next house.

Then she saw Bethany pull up out front and Erin waved at her, motioning to the house and shaking her head. She was trying to tell her that James was home, but Bethany came out of the car, shrugging her shoulders and raising her hands, palms up, indicating she didn't understand.

Erin pointed with her thumb toward the house. She even considered leaving home before James could join them. She was certain that he would much prefer just staying home after the long tour he'd had. Which she should have asked him about. Why was he home so soon? He must have completed his mission.

Bethany's eyes widened as she looked behind Erin. Shoot, Erin's brother was right behind her.

"Hey, Bethany. Hope you don't mind if I join you," James said.

Bethany smiled brightly. "Oh, no, we'll have even more fun."

Erin rolled her eyes. She was hoping Bethany would say she had no more room for him in her car. Then the cad got into the front seat and made Erin sit in back with the cupcakes.

"You know, you can protect *me* all you want," Bethany said. "Erin's got a handle on this."

"I'll protect you both."

Bethany laughed. "Good show. But if you need protecting, I'll be right there for you. How did your trip go?"

"Good. Bad guys are either all dead or turned over to the proper authorities. If I have to return there to take care of them again, I won't be turning them over to the police the next time though."

"I don't blame you. Did Erin tell you she took care of a bank robber today? See? She doesn't need your help." Bethany smiled at James.

Frowning, James glanced over the back seat at Erin, waiting for the whole story.

Erin sighed and explained everything, except she left out one bit of information—the light just dawning. How likely would it be that the musketeer was the guy who broke up her brother and Jane's relationship? A cop on the human police force. A jaguar. Bethany glanced up at the rearview mirror, her brows raised, evidently drawing the same conclusion. So what was the guy doing, if he was the same jaguar, asking her out for a cup of coffee? Unless he'd broken up with Jane already. But it didn't matter. She wasn't going out with someone who had caused the trouble between her brother and his former girlfriend. Then she frowned. He surely wasn't going to be at their party tonight, was he?

"Oh, and by the way, they're doing portraits for the Halloween party this time. So if you're not going to wear a costume, you can strip and shift, and be my very big, black, kitty-cat familiar," Erin said to her brother. They hadn't had family portraits in forever, so this would have to do.

"And Erin and I are going to get photos of us together, witch sisters, you know, and you can sit between us as our shared black jaguar familiar." Bethany turned down another country road.

Erin smiled.

"Works for me. I'll just show my growly side," James said, sounding growly.

The ladies laughed. Erin loved her brother, and she loved it when he could play along with the game. It was just his macho, overprotectiveness that drove her crazy. She just hoped that if Bryce was the one who had broken up her brother's relationship with Jane, he wasn't there tonight.

***

Because so many jaguars were attending the party, they had to park a long distance from the house that was way out in the country, the perfect place for jaguars to live so they could go on a prowl whenever they wanted to. The party was hosted by a brother and sister who were Guardian agents, who took care of injured jaguars, or those who needed to be transported to families to be cared for. They were always off for Halloween so they could host the annual party. That had to do with their Guardian boss always getting invited, and so he made sure they were off the duty schedule for the special occasion.

Paper luminaria bags lighted their driveway all the way to the house. The two-story, colonial brick home was decorated with bats, orange lights, ghosts, jack-o'-lanterns, even hers and Bethany's, spiderwebs, and owls, looking beautifully spooky. She and Bethany and a number of Guardian agents and JAG agents had helped decorate for Halloween, but she hadn't known how beautiful it would look at night.

A black and red dragon—as tall as the ladies—growled as they drew close, its eyes glowing red, smoke coming out of its mouth full of wicked-looking teeth. She loved this time of year.

It was cold out, the fall leaves sporting a full burst of color: orange, red, yellows, purple, with a backdrop of the ever-dependable evergreens of holly, boxwood, and pine trees.

As soon as she and her brother and Bethany entered the house, they were greeted by several JAG, Guardian, and Enforcer agents. Even a couple of JAG agents from the newly-formed United Shifter Force, a combination of jaguars and wolves, were there. Even their JAG boss, Martin, was there. The Enforcer agents were the ones who strictly took down rogue jaguars and others who were murderers. They couldn't allow their kind to end up in prison, concerned they might shift, so they took them down instead.

Erin's boss was no-nonsense when it came to leading the JAG branch, but he was also fun to be around when he let down his hair. He was dressed as Hans Solo, a rebel leader, even though in real life, Martin was always on the right side of the law. Or...almost always, as long as he ensured his people stayed safe. She set the cupcakes with the other treats on the food table.

"Good job on finding those three jaguar poachers and turning them over to the local police in Belize," Martin said to James. "Eliminating the others was a necessary evil, unfortunately. I would have preferred that you turned them all over to the local police to handle, but I know when they're trying to kill you and you're outnumbered, you don't have much of a choice."

"Thanks, boss."

"You know, you have to wear a costume for this event." Martin was always a stickler for propriety. Rules were rules. Even if it was just a party held by some of the agents for fun.

"Yeah, so my sister tells me. I'm going to get something to eat and drink and then I'll prowl around as a jaguar and protect everyone."

Martin laughed and saluted him with his bottle of beer. "Go for it."

Good. Her brother wasn't going to watch her the whole night through.

Bethany immediately began telling their boss about Erin and the bank robbery. Even about the musketeer who was an off-duty cop and jaguar. It didn't hurt that Erin's boss would know that she was doing some off-duty work herself to save the day, as long as it ended with the bad guys going to jail and the good guys being safe.

"You wouldn't be talking about Bryce Jenkins, would you?" Martin asked.

That's when Erin saw Jane with Bryce talking to each other across the party room. So he *was* the man who had broken up her brother and his girlfriend.

"Yeah, one and the same." Erin hoped her brother didn't chew on the guy for being here again once he shifted, though she wanted to march up to Bryce and give him a piece of her mind herself.

***

Wearing his musketeer's outfit, complete with his red cape, shiny sword, and plumed hat, Bryce watched as Erin visited with her friends and he wished *he* could visit with her in the worst way. But he suspected she thought he was dating Jane, when he wasn't, yet he had no other way to get an invitation to the agent-only and significant others' party. He hadn't realized she was the same woman as he'd seen at the JAG training, until he saw her name on her business card after the bank robbery and finally put two and two together.

Jane was a friend, and she had let on that they were dating, so Bryce could come, since she'd dumped her previous boyfriend, James Hawkins, brother to the woman he was interested in! And James was being his growly self, only in jaguar form now. He glanced in Bryce's direction, showed off his teeth, and sauntered off.

Dressed as a lady of the Elizabethan Era, Jane smiled at Bryce. "If you want to talk to Erin, you'd better make it quick. I know I told you her brother was out on a mission, but it appears he handled it and he's returned home. He wouldn't risk getting kicked off the force if he tangled with you tonight though. Erin's going outside to have pictures taken with her girlfriend right now."

"I should have had someone else invite me to the party last year, so it wouldn't appear that you broke up with James to date me." Even though Bryce hadn't met Erin in person until the bank incident, Jane had said nothing but good things about her and how he should try to meet her.

Jane smiled. "You are a 'civilian' as in not one of the jaguar policing force. I'm the only one you're friends with on the force. Too bad she didn't invite you to the party tonight instead when you met her at the bank. It wouldn't have hurt my feelings if you'd gone with her. So you're stuck with me if you want to have a chance to meet her here."

He was fairly certain Erin wouldn't be interested in him now, thinking that he had caused the breakup. Beyond that, Bryce didn't work for the jaguar policing agency, and he assumed Erin might want to find a mate among one of the people she worked with.

Bryce reminded himself he had his heart set on being a homicide detective, and he was nearly there.

With a bottle of beer in hand, he headed outside to see if he could speak with Erin. If he told her he wasn't dating Jane, would Erin even believe him?

Erin was having fun having pictures taken with her friend, Bethany. The two witches were sexy and cute.

He thought, as soon as the witches finished having their Halloween pictures taken, he'd approach Erin, but then her growly brother came along and sat between the two witches who were standing behind a stack of pumpkins for photo ops. The black jaguar gave him a fearsome, snarly look. Bryce couldn't help but smile a little at him. He could give the jaguar just as fearsome a look right back when he was in his jaguar coat. Though he had to admit James's black coat did make the cat look angry and ready to kill.

Erin and James's boss joined Bryce and pointed his beer bottle at the two witches and the jaguar. "I'm kind of surprised you came back to the party this year after breaking up Jane and James's relationship."

"I didn't break them up," Bryce said, figuring if he was going to get thrown out of here, fine. He wanted to clear the air. "Jane invited me because she's the only way I can come to the party. We've been friends for years. Since we were little, actually."

Martin glanced at Bryce and raised a brow. "Hell, you're interested in Erin?"

"Yeah."

Martin laughed. Then he sobered. "I heard about the bank robbery. Good job, both of you. But I don't want you to get into it with James. I like him."

"I didn't cause their breakup," Bryce repeated. "She didn't want to date him any longer. She hasn't been seeing anyone. She just needed her space. She just wasn't ready to settle down and from what she told me, James was looking at marrying her."

"Both Erin and James think otherwise, as far as the breakup is concerned. Just don't start a fight here, or you won't ever be coming back," Martin promised.

Bryce knew Martin was a stern and fair boss, and he looked out for his agents. Yet, Bryce didn't know what came over him to say, "If you're ever looking for another agent..." He let his words trail off.

Martin stared at him for a moment, then smiled. "I thought you were going to make homicide detective soon."

"I was. I mean, I am."

Martin's smile broadened. "So you're thinking of joining us just so you can see Erin?"

"Hell, yeah."

"You don't even know her."

"Jane tells me everything she's done with her job, the times she's worked with her. I was completely impressed with the way she handled the bank robber, and she seems really nice. There may not be anything there, but I want to give it a shot. But then I have this issue with her brother."

"All right. I'll introduce the two of you. Her brother might be standing there growling at you, but he won't bite. Not at least while I'm standing here. And if you and Erin hit it off, she can invite you to the party next year."

"What about a job with the agency?"

"I know your track record. The fact you're ready to become a homicide detective speaks volumes about you. And you helped her out when she took care of the one bank robber. She couldn't have taken care of two on her own. Why don't you see how things go between you and Erin first before you give up your other career? But if you really do want to join us, I wouldn't have any trouble signing you on."

Feeling relieved that Martin thought enough of him to hire him, Bryce nodded. Now the big hurdle was proving to Erin and her brother that he and Jane were just friends and had never been dating. Erin and he might not even hit it off. What then? He supposed he could continue to do what he planned. Take the job as a homicide detective. Yet there was the allure of being a JAG agent and helping other jaguars out and working with fellow jaguars.

Erin's friend Bethany moved out of the picture so that Erin and her brother could get a few alone, her beautiful purple hair flying in the breeze and her brother giving Bryce another snarly growl.

Martin chuckled. Bethany came to see the two of them, and said, "Hey, boss, thanks for giving us the time off for Halloween this year."

"You deserved it. You and Erin had hard missions to complete. Have you met Bryce?" Martin asked.

"Yeah, I mean, not really, but he broke up Jane and James."

"Jane broke up with James," Bryce corrected her, shaking his head. Man, he would never live that down. "She and I are just platonic friends. We've never dated. She's like a sister to me. I gave her a warning and not a ticket some years ago when she was seventeen and speeding. But we'd been friends much earlier than that."

"Oh," Bethany said and glanced back at Erin. "Don't tell me you're interested in meeting Erin."

"Yeah. Except I have to get around her growly brother."

"Which is why the boss is here protecting you?" Bethany asked, smiling.

"I've offered him a job, if he wants it," Martin said.

"Ohmigod." Bethany laughed. "Cat fur is going to fly. I was going to get something to eat and drink, but I think I'll hang around a little longer to see what goes down."

Erin and her brother finished their photo session and Bryce couldn't believe how nervous he felt about seeing her. She was frowning at him, yet he could see in her blue eyes, she knew something was up—the way her boss and best friend were standing with him. She hesitated to join them, glancing at her brother, as if checking to see if he was going to attack Bryce first. Her brother appeared to be waiting for her to make the first move.

She headed for them then, and Bryce was reminded that she was a JAG agent, fearless in her job, and dealing with the man who caused the breakup between her brother and Jane would be an easy task. Her darkened eyes were focused on him, her look as growly as her brother's.

"I'm Bryce Jenkins, we met earlier during the bank robbery, and I'm going to be joining the JAG branch." He didn't know what made him say the words when he had every intention of clearing up the issue on how he wasn't dating Jane, first, and to see if he and Erin could even make a go of it.

Martin chuckled and shook his head.

"I didn't break your brother and Jane up. I've never dated her in my life. I swear it. We've just been friends, like a brother and sister. That's why she invited me to the Halloween party, only she didn't tell me she was breaking up with James that night. So it made it look like I was dating her instead. But it's not like that at all. In truth, she hasn't been dating anyone else since the breakup."

Erin glanced at her brother. He grunted.

"Okay, now that's straightened out, I'm off to enjoy the rest of the party tonight," Martin said, and headed back inside for some more refreshments.

Bryce was hoping the growly jaguar would leave, but he looked intent on staying by his sister's side.

"You're really joining the JAG branch?" Erin asked, sounding astounded, but just a little bit interested too and that gave Bryce hope that he and she could have a few dates, maybe lots more than that.

CHAPTER 3

Surprised at the turn of events concerning Bryce and Jane, Erin and Bryce went in to get some wine, her brother tagging along, annoying her. But then their boss got a call, and Erin was afraid of what that meant. Someone was in trouble.

Sure enough, Martin's brow furrowed. "I'll send some agents right away."

Her brother growled, indicating he was ready to go.

"You just got back from your mission," Martin said to James.

"I'll go with him," Bryce said, surprising Erin, though if he were trying to make brownie points with her, he was earning them.

"You aren't even on the payroll," Martin said.

Erin was sure Martin would put him on the payroll to account for his work with them, if Bryce was allowed to go.

Then again, he was a cop, so Martin couldn't stop him. She figured Bryce could be a tremendous asset for them.

"I'll go." Erin didn't know what came over her to say so when she'd really needed a break.

Bethany nodded. "Me too."

"You don't even know what the assignment is yet," Martin said, frowning at them. "And you two just got off a mission also. Are all my agents workaholics?"

No one else volunteered to go since there were already four of them that had, and though Martin could assign any of his agents who were at the party tonight, he knew it was always better to send ones who were eager to do the job.

"We have a family of jaguars who have had a break-in. Their home is near here. They have three children who are two-years old."

James had already left to shift and dress.

Bethany said, "I've got a gun in the car."

"I have one in mine," Bryce said. "And a sword." He patted his sword.

Martin handed his gun to Erin. "Be sure to bring it back in good working order."

She saluted him, and, surprising her, Jane gave James her gun. No one better ever try to come here to rob them at a shifter Halloween party. They'd be dead meat.

"Human robbers?" Erin asked Martin as he followed them out to the vehicles.

"Human. The jaguar family only managed a call to me. They were afraid to call the police and have them botch the job. We use a lot more stealth," Martin said.

Erin prayed they could rescue the family without any of them getting hurt. The husband and wife weren't agency cats, so they weren't trained like the agents were for taking down enemies in a hostile situation.

Bethany was driving her car and Erin went with her, while her brother rode with Bryce in his truck. She suspected James was going to give him the third degree about Jane.

"What do you think about his story? Bryce, I mean?" Bethany asked, as a way to lighten the tension-filled mood they were both feeling, hoping everything would turn out the way they wanted it to. "*I* believe his story. Anyone who would face-down your growly brother in his jaguar form has my vote. Besides, the jaguar is a hot musketeer."

"I agree about Bryce's story. He wouldn't have any reason to lie, or he could easily get caught up in it. And Bryce didn't face down my brother only because Martin was making my brother behave either. Bryce came over to watch us long before that."

"Are you going to date the guy? I mean, anyone who would make such a drastic career change in hopes of seeing a she-cat who is in the same branch as him has to be rather...intriguing to you. Not to mention he helped you out with taking the bank robbers down. I keep visualizing the two of you, you in your witch's costume kicking butt and him swinging his sword as a musketeer."

Erin smiled. "Yeah, that had to have looked like a movie scene." She wondered if anyone in the bank had managed to capture video of it. It seemed nowadays everyone recorded a video for everything. She checked her phone. Sure enough, there she was kneeing the guy in the jewels and she got to see how swiftly Bryce moved, first ensuring she had the guy under control that she was dealing with, before he sprinted to take down the other guy, who was aiming to shoot at her, but hesitated, looking as though he was afraid he'd hit his partner. And then Bryce was swinging his sword, striking the robber's gun just right to knock it out of his hand. Bryce looked like he must have had lessons as precise as his movements were.

"I have to admit no one has ever offered to leave a job just so he could date me. You don't think he had too many beers tonight, do you?"

"No. He was nursing the one beer the whole time." Bethany glanced at Erin's phone. "Video of the action?"

"Yep, in living color."

"Cool. I'll have to watch it after we get this situation under control. Bryce seemed really friendly the last time I saw him. Friendly in an agreeable way, not that he was looking to date someone at the time, just that he was enjoying being around other jaguars at a party. You know, it has to be hard to work with a human police force and all your friends are...well, human. It's nice being around our own kind so we can talk about business and jaguar issues."

"True." Erin took a deep breath and exhaled it, preparing herself for the fight ahead that she was certain they would face.

It took them about ten more minutes to reach the home that was out in the country like the other. Big blown-up Halloween decorations, the cute kind for their little ones, Erin imagined, were lit by lights, bringing Halloween cheer to the house. It made Erin feel bad about what was going on inside the house. She prayed they were able to get in before these creeps did anything to hurt any of the family members.

As soon as they parked way out, they saw a van sitting in the driveway. When the rest of their team joined them, Bryce said, "I've got my badge on me."

Erin glanced at his musketeer costume. At least he had ditched his beautiful cape and plumed hat, but he still didn't look much like a police officer. He was still wearing his sword, which might come in handy, like it had earlier today.

"If we have to, we take them down permanently," James growled.

"Yeah, of course," Bryce said. "No argument with you there."

Then they all split up and moved toward the house. James indicated he was going around the back side of the two-story home. Bethany went to the east and Erin went to the west while Bryce was wearing his badge, heading for the front door.

As soon as Erin reached the side window that looked into the laundry room, she tried the window and found it unlocked. She whistled low to let the others know she found a way in, if they hadn't. She didn't wait for anyone though and pushed up the window as slowly as she could. Before she could move some logs over so that she could climb into the window, Bryce was there, helping her up, his hands securely on her hips. Then she slid in, trying to avoid a wastepaper basket full of dryer lint beneath the window and landed softly on the floor. She quickly moved the wastepaper basket out of the way. The door was closed to the laundry room, but she could hear a woman and kids crying in the direction of what she suspected was the living room, while the mom was trying to shush them through her sobs.

"I'm not going to ask you again. Where's your safe?" a deep-voiced male said.

"I-I don't have a safe," the homeowner said. "I told you that already. I gave you what cash we had."

Erin slowly opened the door and heard Bryce move in right behind her. She hoped Bethany and James were either coming or had found other places to safely enter the house.

She pushed the door open wider, listening to hear where everyone was. She heard someone upstairs, the family in the living room, a man with them there, and someone else down the hall from where she was.

Then she heard a slight thump behind her and turned to see her brother in jaguar form leaping through the window into the laundry room and landing on the tile floor. She motioned to the stairs up on her right and moved out of his way, so he could take care of the vermin upstairs.

They needed to get rid of whoever was down the hall too. She hoped there were only three men, but then she heard someone getting something out of the fridge. She suspected the family wasn't eating at a time like this.

Bryce whispered to her, "I'll take out the man down the hall. Wait here for the rest of us to take out the others. Sounds like there may be two more."

She nodded. If she hadn't worried her actions could hurt the family, she would have gone in shooting, just to take the men down before they could injure or kill anyone. But there were at least two more culprits and she didn't want to provoke them into shooting the family.

She heard someone cry out upstairs and a thump down the hall sounded from the direction where Bryce had gone. She hoped he'd taken the bad guy out and not the other way around, but if the bad guy had knocked out Bryce, she was certain he would have shouted they had company.

Instead, a man rushed out of the kitchen, gun in hand. At that point, she couldn't wait. When he saw her, she didn't have any choice but to shoot him before he could hit her. She fired two shots, and he went down. It appeared she'd killed him. But they still had another man in the living room with the family.

Her brother tore down the stairs as a jaguar, and he looked fiercer than she'd ever seen him. She knew the man in the living room wouldn't hesitate to shoot the jaguar. She thought he wouldn't try to use one of the family as a shield against a jaguar, not like he would against someone armed with a gun. Her brother had the right idea. And even if the perp did use someone as a hostage, her brother would aim the deadly swipe of his paw at the shooter's head and kill him that way.

Even so, she rushed forth to help rescue the rest of the family and get them out of harm's way.

Shots were fired outside, and Erin realized Bethany was still out there. Someone must have tried to get away. Erin recognized the sound of the gunfire. Only Bethany got any rounds off. Erin was glad she had stayed outside to get the last of the culprits, *if* that was the last of them.

Bryce was right beside Erin as they bolted into the living room.

The mom and kids were terrified that her husband was being held as a shield against the swipes of the angry jaguar. Erin swept up two of the kids and hollered at the mother, "Come with me. How many of them are there?"

"Four men and a woman."

Erin rushed the mom, who was carrying one of the crying triplets, and the other kids down the hall, out of harm's way in case the robber's gun went off and struck the kids or mother accidentally *or* on purpose. "Stay here."

Erin hurried back to the living room to see her brother trying to reach the robber as he kept the homeowner in front of him. Bryce fired two shots, one that struck the robber's arm and he dropped his gun, and the other round hit the robber in the head. He dropped to the floor, dead.

They had to kill them all. The men would have told the police they had seen a jaguar in the house. And if someone had investigated the crime scene to see if he'd been telling the truth, they would have found lots of jaguar fur in the house, proving what the men said was true.

Even so, they would have had to come up with a story about how the man upstairs had been killed by a single blow to the head, when no one had used a weapon on him.

Before Bryce reported any of this to the police, he and James went outside to check on Bethany and make sure there were no more robbers in the area who just hadn't been in the house at the time. Erin checked over the family to make sure they were all right. They were terrified, which was understandable, but no injuries, thank God.

Erin got on her phone after the family was all situated on the couch. "Martin, the family is safe." She explained how it all had gone down. "How do you want to handle this?"

"We'll clean it up. We could try to explain how you had saved the day, but I'm sure it will be easier to just make it all go away. I'll send in a cleanup team. I'll call in a Guardian team to take the family in for the next couple of days while we clean everything up."

"Thank you." She relayed the information to the family as her brother, Bethany, and Bryce rejoined them in the house. Erin was glad the cleanup wasn't part of their job description. Just taking out the bad guys was. Or arresting them, if they could. In this case, it just wasn't feasible. Sure, her brother could have gone up the stairs as a human, but he hadn't made a sound as a jaguar, and so he had the element of surprise. If any of them had walked up the stairs as humans, he could have made the steps creak, alerting the gunman that someone was sneaking up there and he could have fired on her brother before he had even made it to the landing upstairs. And that would have alerted the other robbers to come out shooting.

They waited with the family until the Guardian agents would arrive, a married couple who took in jaguar families in crisis. The Guardians had lots of counseling training, so they could help the family overcome the ordeal. In the meantime, Bethany and Erin cuddled with two of the kids in their arms, while their mom rocked the third toddler in hers. Dad had gone upstairs to wash up and change clothes because he was wearing the blood of the man Bryce had shot and killed.

The family was grateful to them, and Erin was so relieved they had saved their lives. Once the Guardian agents had arrived, they helped everyone to pack, then carried the family away in a van. Another two vans showed up with the cleaning teams to get rid of all the vermin and evidence left behind shortly after that. Their job done, Erin and Bethany headed back to the party in her car. James, who had shifted and dressed, rode back with Bryce.

Everyone was ready to enjoy the rest of their Halloween, and Erin had wished she'd truly been a powerful witch so she could have used some spells to get rid of the bad guys in a more interesting way. But she knew, that no matter how much fun she might be having at the party, when shifters were in trouble, she would drop everything to rescue them. She really respected Bryce too, for his handling of the situation, both with regard to protecting her brother and the jaguar the robber had held hostage. And earlier, at the bank too. She was glad, now that she knew he hadn't been the cause of James and Jane's breakup, that Bryce was joining the JAG branch. She hoped Martin would let her work with him too.

***

"Hey, thanks, man, for not shooting me back there," James said to Bryce as they drove back to the house.

Bryce cast him a sardonic smile. "It wouldn't have done me any good when I want to date your sister."

"You really never dated Jane?"

"Not a day in my life. She's just a good friend. We've been friends since we were kids. She thought I should come to the party last year to meet others like us who are also into policing the bad guys. I didn't know she was planning to breakup with you. I've always thought I could help our kind by being on a human police force, but last year when I went to the party with Jane, I started to see things differently. Like, how much I wanted to be with our kind, the comradery you all have as both jaguars and a police force." He motioned his arm in the direction of the house they were leaving. "And things like this. Working together as a team, a jaguar force to be reckoned with, aiding others of the shifter kind. Hell, wearing a jaguar coat while taking out the bad guys. I never imagined doing that in the line of duty."

"Yeah, it's one of the perks of being a jaguar." James paused. "Since you're such good friends with Jane, did she tell you why she broke up with me?"

"Only that she wasn't ready to settle down and you seemed to be much more interested in rushing into it. Hell, I don't know. Women are a mystery to me."

James laughed. "They sure as hell are."

"So you don't mind me dating your sister?" Not that Bryce felt he had to ask permission of Erin's brother, so he wasn't sure why he asked. Though he probably did so because he was going to be working with them and he wanted to get started off on the right foot.

"Not that I have any control over what my sister does or doesn't do, but as long as she wants to, I don't have any problem with it. Just don't tell her you asked me first."

Bryce smiled.

When they returned to the party, several said they were glad they'd resolved the trouble without any of the family being injured and the agents and the police officer had been safe. The party had been at a standstill while everyone waited to hear if reinforcements had been needed to be sent to the family's house.

Salutes and drinks were offered to the agents and the officer. Then the party resumed. Music began to play and several of the agents began to dance.

"Would you like to dance?" Bryce asked Erin, setting his empty wine glass down on a table.

"Yeah, sure." She noticed that her brother was talking to Jane, and she wondered what that was all about. But what really surprised her was when James began to slow dance with her.

"Looks like Jane and your brother might be getting back together," Bryce said.

"Or not. She might just be showing him some gratitude for taking care of the hostage situation and returning to the party unharmed."

"You believe that as much as I do."

"You're right." It was hard for them to hide their true feelings about another jaguar. They watched for cues, much more aware of body language and facial expressions, not to mention smelling emotions also. Her brother hadn't dated but a few women since the breakup, but only one-date affairs. He was still totally hung up on Jane, even though he didn't mention it to Erin. He didn't need to. All it took was for them to be in the same room together, and he looked so hopeful Jane would say something to him.

Bethany was dancing with an Enforcer agent when James left Jane off at one of the tables of food and came over to speak to Erin.

"Hey, tell Bethany that I'm going home with Jane," James said.

Erin couldn't believe it, but she was glad he was getting back together with her, if that's what they both wanted. Unless it didn't work out or this was a one-time deal.

"Okay, sure, I'll tell her."

When James left the party with Jane, Bryce said, "Bethany doesn't have to drop you off at home either. I can take you."

"Why, how sweet of you. Would you mind if we stop by the grocery store on the way home? I need to pick up some milk and a new broom."

Bryce smiled at her witch's costume. "A new broom, eh?"

She laughed. "You don't want to know what happened to the last one."

He just raised his brows and smiled, looking as though he really did want to know. "I'll be giving two weeks' notice at my job on Monday. Martin said I'd be in training for a couple of weeks after that. I thought if you weren't on assignment in the meantime, we could go out."

They danced nice and slow to the music and she thought he had some winning moves, both when he went after villains and with her.

"Sure. Would you like to go to the zoo tomorrow?"

"The zoo?" He sounded so amazed she wanted to laugh.

"I hear there's a new black jaguar in the zoo and I want to check it out—just to make sure it's the real deal and not one of our kind."

Bryce looked surprised to hear she thought it might be a shifter. "Has that ever happened before?"

"Once. Except that time, he was a wolf. When I saw him, I confused him. Of course, I didn't expect the wolf to be a shifter. But I smelled like a jaguar to him, and I wasn't in a uniform, indicating I worked at the zoo. The wolf wouldn't have acted the way he did toward me, if he'd been a regular wolf. I called my boss and said I believed we had a wolf shifter locked up in the zoo. As soon as I said that, the wolf nodded. He kept his focus on me the whole time. I told my boss the wolf was for sure a shifter. I swore he wanted to shift right then and there to prove it. We had way too much company at the time."

"So what did you do?"

"We got a 'federal' search warrant to check the wolf out. And then we showed 'proof' that the wolf was stolen. We transferred him out of there and took him to a safe house. Guardian agents brought him clothes to wear and located his car. He'd been a missing person for two weeks, but the police hadn't been notified because he'd been on vacation. Which was probably a good thing, considering he was a wolf shifter. All he could hope for was somehow making it out of the zoo on his own, or alerting a shifter visiting the zoo that he was one too. Poor guy.

"He'd been chasing after a female wolf, he thought might need his protection—wolfish guy—and he ended up falling into a pit that he couldn't get out of. He'd broken a leg."

"Ouch."

"Yeah, and it was winter, so he had to remain in his wolf coat to protect himself from the cold. He thought he could howl for the wolf and maybe her pack, if she lived with one in the area. Though he'd never seen any sign of any. But men came and found him, not wolf shifters, and they took him to the zoo so that he could be patched up. He'd been terrified that they might think they needed to put him to sleep, permanently, but they set his leg and he healed up quickly. He was so well-behaved around people, like he'd been a pet dog, that they were afraid he might have been raised by someone, and that he wouldn't be able to live in the wild on his own. Not only that, but no regular wolves live in the area, so they figured he couldn't have been wild."

Bryce shook his head. "He was damn lucky that you came along then. What happened to the female?"

"No sign of her, though we searched for her scent."

"You have a good nose for helping others out. I bet he was grateful to you for securing his release. I can't imagine getting caught and stuck in a zoo. So you really do go to the zoo to see if a shifter has been stuck in there accidentally."

"Yep. Besides, I love seeing the animals."

"I'm always up for a trip to the zoo. Especially if it means rescuing fellow shifters. Now, about your broom…?"

She laughed. "Come on. Let's go before the store closes." She told Bethany that Bryce was taking her home.

Bethany's expression brightened. "My, my, the bewitching night has brought some special magic to the party, I see."

"We're going on our first official date tomorrow. The zoo."

Bethany laughed. "Have you told him what happened the last time you went to the zoo?"

"Yeah, he's ready to climb into the enclosure and free the jaguar."

Bryce laughed. "With you at my back, I can do anything."

CHAPTER 4

"I saw you in training once," Bryce told Erin as he drove her to the grocery store, glad she'd agreed to have him take her home.

"Martin knew that you were there?" Erin sounded surprised.

He didn't blame her. Training was only for the agents working for the organization, not for outsiders to witness.

"Yeah. Jane was training too and she got permission from your boss. I think he suspected if I saw all the comradery of the jaguars in training, I might decide to join the force. I met Martin a couple of years ago, when I stopped him for a taillight that was out. I was as surprised to learn he was a jaguar as much as he was surprised to learn that I was. He said, back then, that if I ever was interested in a job, to come look him up. I came to watch Jane, primarily, but then you caught my eye. You were a blond then."

Erin smiled.

"You went on a mission right after the training and Jane didn't know if you'd be back in time for the Halloween party. But I'd wanted to meet you. I didn't recognize you at the bank when your hair was a pretty purple. I hadn't been anywhere near you to smell your scent to get to know you that way when you were in training."

"What did you see me do at my training that made you want to get to know me better?"

"You were trying to take down a jaguar in the water, like you would do if you had to eliminate a shifter in the jungle who was in his jaguar form. I have to admit that's not something I'd get to do as a cop. You had me intrigued. Especially when you came out on top."

"You'll have to take real jungle warfare training too."

"I've been to a number of the locations where you have to deal with jaguar trouble south of the border. Not that I was there for anything more than vacations to stretch out my legs as a jaguar in our native environment, but I did have to deal with some drug runners once. As a jaguar. Though our kind, the non-shifting kind, I should say, don't hunt humans normally, as shifters, our jaguar form is perfect for hunting the bad guys."

"I agree. It gets trickier when the ones you're after are jaguar shifters too."

Bryce finally pulled into a parking lot at the grocery store. "I'm still curious about you needing a new broom."

"You won't believe it, but I was cleaning spiderwebs off the eaves of my roof, though I should have left them up for Halloween decorations, and when I began to step down, a neighbor's friendly, black cat jumped on the ladder. I lost my balance when I couldn't step down or I would have stepped on Jinx. Anyway, somehow, I managed not to kill myself, but I broke the broom when I landed."

He chuckled. "I'm glad you didn't hurt yourself."

"Well, darn cat wouldn't move. You'd think he would have jumped out of the way, but nope. Luckily, with our own springy cat reactions, I was able to land okay, the only casualty—the broom."

Bryce laughed.

After picking up a broom and some milk at the store, she and Bryce returned to the car.

He dropped her off at her house, and she thanked him for the ride. "Do you want me to pick you up to go to the zoo tomorrow morning?" she asked.

"I was going to offer, but it's up to you. Either way is good for me."

"I'll pick you up."

He gave her his address, and then he hoped for a kiss, but she smiled and said good-night and headed inside the house.

He hoped that they'd hit it off. It would be nice to work with the JAG branch when he was already friends with some of the jaguars. And it would really be nice if he got to date Erin. She was fun and courageous and determined to take down those who threatened others and protect those who couldn't protect themselves.

He sure hadn't been this interested in a she-cat in years.

Once he arrived home, he stripped off his musketeer costume and took a shower, thinking about how he hadn't been to a zoo since he was a little kid. He was looking forward to it. He couldn't even imagine one of their own kind being incarcerated there. He hoped it was just a regular jaguar, that she'd be agreeable to dinner later that night...and a kiss.

***

When Erin arrived to pick him up the next morning, Bryce was ready for a fun-filled day. Here he'd thought he was going to be sitting at home, watching TV or something. He was glad to have real plans today, especially when it meant spending the day with Erin.

She was wearing jeans, boots, and a long-sleeved shirt, her hair back to being blond.

"Looks like you shifted sometime after I left you. I thought you might still have purple hair today."

"I wanted to go for a jaguar run after all the food we ate last night."

"I could have gone with you."

"Tonight, if you'd like."

"Sure, that would be great. Dinner out and we can return to either my place or yours and run," he said, glad they were going to do more together than just visit the zoo.

"I'd love that."

They finally reached the zoo, found a parking space, and he was surprised, but shouldn't have been when she gave him a free pass because she was a member of the zoo. "To check for shifters all year long when I have a chance," she said.

He wondered if it was that or she just liked to see all the animals at the zoo.

They entered the zoo and he had every intention of letting her choose what she wanted to see first, beyond checking out the big cat. But he truly wanted to see the bears and the other big cats too.

They walked to the big cat exhibits first and found the black jaguar. There was no way to tell if it was a shifter from just looking at it. The jaguar was lying on top of a log and staring at them.

"Come talk to us," Erin called out to it, ignoring that other visitors to the zoo were observing the beautiful jaguar.

Bryce was watching for any indication the jaguar was showing signs that he was one of them. He expected it to leap down from the log and come closer, to chuff in their way, to do anything that would show he realized they were one of his kind.

"Okay, then you're not one of us," she finally said, when most of the visitors had moved on to the next exhibit. Still she waited, just in case the cat indicated he was a shifter too. He didn't.

Bryce waited patiently with her, observing the cat for any indication he was a shifter. "He wouldn't have any reason to hide what he was from us, I wouldn't think."

"He's not one of us. The wolf came over immediately to try and communicate with me the best he could." Then she said to the cat, "You're beautiful though." Then she took Bryce's hand and led him through the big cat exhibits to see the lions, tigers, cougars, and outside, another jaguar, golden in color. "Hello, beautiful cat. She's been here for a couple of years, so not one of us. Where to next?"

"Bears?"

She smiled. "I love the bears. We can check to see if they have any more wolves too."

They ended up seeing everything at the zoo, stopping to eat some tacos at a rain forest café, and then they went to the aquarium. "If I wasn't a big cat, I wouldn't mind being a dolphin," she said.

"Me? Something that flies. Though I prefer being a big cat. It would be easier to hide what we are from the rest of the population if we were wolves though."

"Sure, if people thought we were dogs, I agree. I watched a program once where people were keeping tigers, but one escaped. This man was just getting out of his car when he saw the tiger approach him at his home. He hurried inside and called the police. If someone saw a wolf, most likely they'd think it was a dog. A tiger? What a shock, and scary too. When he called the police to report a tiger was running through his property, they didn't believe it until they checked the paw prints in the mud. And eventually, they had other sightings and located it. Luckily, the tiger didn't kill anyone, which is the real concern."

"I agree. Hey, I gather from what your boss said, you're on vacation for a couple of weeks. Did you want to go on a ride-along with me and my partner tomorrow?"

"Sure, and watch you do your job as a human cop?"

"Yeah. But you'll just be an observer."

She pulled out her badge. "I serve and protect too and if you need backup, I'll be there."

"That's true. It's up to us to let you go with us on a job, if we need more help. Since you're authorized to carry a gun in your law enforcement work, you can carry one when you go with us."

"All right, sure. I'd like to do that." She got a call and said, "Hey, yeah, James?" She smiled. "Sure, okay. If she's wanting you to back off on setting down roots, then... Good. I'm glad for you both. See you later."

"Is that about Jane and James?" Bryce asked.

"Yeah. My brother is moving back in with her. My brother is really a family guy, so I think he was pushing for a commitment and she just wasn't ready. But it sounds like their separation from each other for the year hadn't stopped her interest in him anymore than he'd given up on her. Though he did see you as an obstacle to their getting together again."

"Not me. Never me. Sure, we went to the movies or out to dinner when neither of us were dating, but it wasn't a date. Just like if I'd gone out with the guys. I'm glad they're getting back together. Jane hasn't been her cheerful, happy-go-lucky self since they broke up." Their getting together again worked well for Bryce, he thought, if her brother had a she-cat to take up his time and wasn't monitoring Bryce's dates with Erin. Though Bryce hoped it worked out this time and they didn't break up again. "So what would you like for dinner?"

"Pizza?"

"Pizza it is."

They left the zoo and drove to her favorite pizza place, which happened to be his also. In fact, he was such a regular here, everyone knew him. She'd just learned of it, or he might have run into her there, sometime or another.

"Hey, Officer Jenkins, you're back. Same as usual?" Joey, one of the pizza employees said.

"Yep, same kind of pizza."

"And for the lovely lady?"

She watched the man throw red sauce, cheese, spinach leaves, pepperoni, mushrooms, red and green bell peppers, and tomatoes on Bryce's pizza. "Same as he's having. Looks good."

"Yes, ma'am."

It didn't take long for the pizzas to be done, and they were enjoying their dinner in a booth.

"So what's your favorite animal?" she asked, separating a slice of pizza from the rest and lifting it to her lips?

"Jaguar. You have to ask? She-cat variety. You, actually."

She smiled. "Did you learn how to wield a sword on your own or did you take training for it?"

"Training, martial arts. I never knew it would actually come in handy when trying to take down a bank robber though."

"I was impressed. I like your choice of pizza too. My brother eats all meat and only meat on his pizza. You'd think he was a jaguar or something."

Bryce chuckled. "My mother convinced me that as humans it was good to eat fruits and vegetables also. Or no dessert."

Erin laughed.

After they finished dinner, she drove them back to his place and they stripped off their clothes inside, then shifted and ran out through the pet door.

He didn't want the night to end as much as he was enjoying the time spent with Erin. She seemed to be having just as much fun or she probably would have dropped him off and gone on her way tonight.

They ran through the woods, chasing each other, leaping into trees, and down the other side, swatting each other's tails, then tackling each other in fun. Man, he could really get used to runs with the she-cat. He'd run with his police partner a few times but running with a wolf wasn't the same. Jack couldn't climb trees and Bryce certainly hadn't wanted to tackle him and accidentally injure him.

She rubbed up against Bryce in friendship and intimacy.

And then she headed for his place. Once they arrived there, shifted, and dressed, she kissed him and headed for the door. "See you tomorrow?"

He was going to offer her some coffee or something before she left, but he didn't want to be like James was with Jane, and push Erin too much too fast.

Even so, he caught her hand before she could leave, pulled her against his body, and kissed her, slowly, surely, deepening the kiss. She wrapped her arms around his waist and kissed him right back, as if she hadn't wanted to seem too needy, but when he forced the issue, she was just as willing. But then she finally pulled away, smiling at him.

"I had a ton of fun. Meet you at the police station tomorrow?"

"Yeah, bright and early."

***

Erin couldn't stop thinking about all the fun she'd had with Bryce and she was super glad that James had moved back in with Jane so that if she needed some more intimate time at her place with Bryce, she'd have it. Or they could spend that time at his place. No matter what, unless things changed drastically between them and he wasn't the cat she thought he was, she wanted to continue dating him.

Bethany called Erin as she was getting ready for bed. She climbed into bed and answered the call.

"Hey, how was it?" Bethany asked.

"We had a ball. The jaguar at the zoo is strictly a jaguar. And Bryce is a fun date."

"Dinner?"

"At my new favorite pizza place."

"And?"

"And a run. I think that was the most fun I've had with a sexy, male jaguar in forever. I love running with you, as you know, but man, he's got some moves."

Bethany laughed. "Okay, just remember to save some time for us to get together."

"We have two weeks before we're both back to work. I'm going on a ride-along with Bryce tomorrow and dinner probably tomorrow night, my treat this time, unless one of us gets shot and can't make it."

"You know how to live dangerously. Okay, the day after, did you want to have lunch out and go shopping?"

"That would be great."

"Perfect. How about that soup and sandwich shop?"

"Sounds great."

"You're alone, right?"

"Uh, yeah. You know I don't shack up with a guy on first dates."

"Or second and third, fourth, maybe fifth. Are you going to help him out if Bryce has any bad cases that he has to handle on his shift tomorrow?"

"Yeah, if he'll let me."

"Okay, I'll let you get your sleep. Let me know how it goes."

"I will. Night, Bethany."

"Night, Erin. Be safe."

Erin set her phone on the charger next to her bed and turned off the light. All she could envision was Bryce smiling down at her, right before he kissed her again. Until she fell asleep and was tackling a robber in her dreams and a musketeer was swinging his sword at the other one.

CHAPTER 5

The next day for the ride-along, Erin drove over to the police station and met up with Bryce and his partner, Jack Wolff. She recognized him instantly. He was the blond-haired man she'd rescued from the zoo last year. She couldn't believe he was a cop! She laughed.

Jack smiled and shook his head at her as they climbed into the police cruiser.

"You two know each other?" Bryce asked, appearing surprised as he climbed into the driver's seat.

"Yeah, you remember the story I told you about the gray wolf in the zoo?" Erin asked.

"No way. That was you, Jack? Get out of here." Bryce chuckled.

"Yeah, unfortunately. Luckily, I was on leave for a couple of weeks while I was incarcerated in the zoo, so the police never knew of it. Until you now."

"I would never divulge your secret. Not to a bunch of human cops. I guess you never caught up with that she-wolf or you would have told me you were dating. Or why you weren't dating."

"No. I never did locate her. She must have been just passing through. I still can't believe you're leaving the force to work with the jaguar police force now. Then again, I would, if I got to work with a shifter like Erin. I mean, if she were a wolf. As to my zoo incarceration, that was not the way I wanted to spend my vacation."

They all laughed.

They ended up doing a number of routine traffic stops for speeding, expired car registration, missing safety inspection, expired safety inspections, but then they got a call about a home invasion.

"Seems to be the time for them," Erin said, thinking about the case where the jaguars' home was invaded last night.

"Yeah, I didn't tell you about that," Bryce told his partner.

They were the closest cops on duty to the location of the home invasion, and on the way over there, Bryce explained to Jack what had happened.

"Hell, sounds like a great organization to work for," Jack said. "What do we do about our ride-along on this case?"

"You want to take me with you, both to help deal with the situation and diffuse it." Erin smiled at Jack.

"She's a keeper," Jack said.

"Yeah, just what I was thinking."

Bryce pulled up in front of the two-story, white-siding house and parked. Then all three of them hurried to leave the patrol car. Shots were fired inside the house and the officers and Erin sprinted for the front door, their guns drawn. Since they healed faster than humans if they were wounded, the shifters tended to take more chances than most humans did when they needed to rescue someone.

Jack radioed that shots had been fired and Bryce tried the doorknob. He turned it and shoved the door open, then jumped aside to make sure that he didn't take a round. Erin couldn't believe that she and Bryce were dealing with another armed robbery at a home. This time, the homeowners were human though.

The officers and Erin rushed into the house and heard a woman and children upstairs in a bedroom crying.

Someone in a room on the first floor was groaning.

Erin motioned to the stairs. She was going up to check on the family, when a man rushed into the house through the front door and Jack and Bryce aimed their guns at him.

"I live here," the man said, holding his hands up in the air.

"Checking on the family," Erin said again and tore up the stairs, wanting to make sure that no one was holding them hostage up there.

Bryce nodded while Jack checked the man for weapons and ID, learned he was the owner of the house, then made him go outside for his own safety. Other police cruisers were pulling up and Jack and Bryce headed for the room where they'd heard the man groaning, and another speaking low, harshly. "Come on, man, we gotta get outta here. We'll deal with Wendell later."

Bryce wasn't sure what they'd find. A wounded family member or one of the housebreakers.

Then Bryce peered into the room and saw a man clutching his chest, another turning his weapon on Bryce. Bryce and Jack hurried into the room, both men shouting to the armed gunman to drop his weapon.

"You haven't shot anyone yet," Bryce said, trying to reason with the gunman. At least he hoped he hadn't shot any of the family members. Even so, the guy could be a wanted felon for any number of other crimes. "And your friend's wounded. Let us take care of him."

"You haven't killed anyone," Jack agreed, both men trying to talk the gunman out of shooting at them.

The gunman set the gun on the floor.

"Shove it over this way," Bryce said, and once the gunman did, he confiscated it.

"Clear up here!" Erin called out.

"Clear down here," Bryce called out to her as he handcuffed the guy.

Jack got on his radio. "Two gunmen. One GSW, self-inflicted, it appears."

Bryce collected the other man's gun resting on the floor on the other side of the room where he must have dropped it when he was hit and Bryce cuffed him.

"Looks like he was trying to open the safe by shooting at it." Bryce motioned with his head to the marks the rounds had made on the steel safe. "It appears two of the rounds ricocheted off the metal safe and struck the would-be robber."

Jack shook his head.

The men were taken into custody and the husband and his wife and two sons were reunited.

"I came home to give the men the combination number for the safe, so they wouldn't kill my family," the husband said, his voice rough with emotion as he hugged his wife and his young boys. "I wouldn't give it to them over the phone, afraid they'd eliminate my wife and sons as soon as they had it."

Bryce noticed the wife seemed perturbed with her husband though, and he wondered what that was all about when she pulled her boys away from the dad and put some distance between them.

After all the statements were taken, Bryce was surprised to learn that the men who attempted the robbery were the homeowner's cousins and the wife told the police about her husband's auto business. She thought that maybe he was flipping cars and that's what this was all about.

Then Bryce and his partner and Erin were finally able to get back on the road.

"I'm glad you didn't have to shoot anybody on the job," Erin said.

"Yeah, it's bad for everyone concerned. Much better if we can talk the men down." Bryce hadn't known what to expect with how the jaguars handled a case.

"We try to talk them down too, if we can. But if we can't, we just handle it," Erin said. "Of course, if it's all just shifters involved, that makes our life easier. You know what the worst part of this armed robbery was?"

"What's that?" Jack asked as they got another call, this time a case of domestic violence.

"Those armed men were family and knew he had lots of cash in there."

"Yeah, they say a good percentage of crimes against people are perpetrated by family, friends, or associates. Not strangers," Bryce said.

"He might have bragged about the money, or they might have been involved in it and felt they needed to get a bigger cut. The wife was furious with whatever underhanded business her husband was involved in. He could have gotten her and the kids killed. She plans to divorce him." Erin sighed. "She might have been passively going along with it as long as no one was the wiser, but once it could mean danger for her and the kids, it was time to fess up."

"I checked on the cousins and they both have priors for car theft. I'd say they were involved in the business. Both were out on parole too," Jack said.

"Maybe this time they'll stay in jail for a while," Bryce said.

Then they started to talk about the domestic abuse case.

"Been to that address a number of times for the same issue," Jack said. "The woman beats up on her husband and he calls 911 when he feels his life is threatened. The thing of it is, he's six-four and she's five-four, and he's hefty, she's petite, so no one puts a whole lot of stock in it."

"Especially when he refuses to press charges," Bryce said.

They arrived at the house where the family was having the dispute and found the wife had stabbed her husband in the chest with a kitchen knife on the front porch. Jack called for backup and an ambulance while Bryce tried to talk the woman down.

"Put the knife down," Bryce ordered.

The woman's eyes were wild with madness.

"I don't want to shoot you. Drop. The. Weapon."

Jack moved in to get the husband out of harm's way and the woman finally dropped the knife. Bryce took her into custody and paramedics arrived and quickly stabilized the husband.

The wife was read her rights and hauled off to jail while the husband was transported to the hospital.

"Since he always drops the charges against his wife, I doubt this will be any different," Jack said when they were finished. "He doesn't want the rest of the world to know his wife beats up on him. Yet, he still calls 911, as if the cops knowing the situation is all right."

"Or maybe because by that time, he's sober and doesn't want to press charges. They were both intoxicated." Erin climbed back into the car.

"That's how it always begins. But this is the first time she's taken a knife to him," Bryce said. "Maybe this time, he'll charge her with battery."

"Is it always this crazy when you pull your shift or is it because of the full moon?" Erin asked.

"Full moon," both Bryce and Jack said.

"Hey, after we're through, did you want to have dinner out tonight?" Bryce asked Erin.

"I've got other plans, but thanks for asking," Jack said.

Erin chuckled. "Yeah, I'd like that. My boss promises me no job calls while I'm off-duty for the next two weeks."

"Okay, good. We can decide where to eat after our shift is over."

When they finally finished their shift and returned to the police station, a couple of the officers asked if she'd ride-along with them next. That they could use her as backup.

Smiling, she knew they meant for more than just police work, but they wouldn't be able to handle a wild cat like her. Bryce and Jack only smiled at the other officers.

"I'll pick you up at seven for dinner?" Bryce asked.

"Okay, see you then." She left in her own car and headed home, glad she was with the jaguar policing force and not with the human one. The police did a necessary job, but she still liked her job better. She hoped Bryce wouldn't miss working on the police force.

As soon as she arrived home, she saw James's car parked in the garage. *Oh no.* Erin hoped that he and Jane hadn't already had a falling out.

She walked into the house, expecting to see her brother pacing in the living room, a beer in hand, but he was in his bedroom, the door open.

"Is everything okay?" she asked.

"Yeah, how does a January wedding sound?"

Erin smiled and entered his bedroom where he was packing up all his clothes. She leaned against the door jamb and folded her arms. "For real? You didn't coerce her to agree to marry you, did you?"

"Nah. She was the one who insisted on it."

Erin raised a brow.

"Truly. She said she needed the time away, but once we were together again, the sparks flew. Uh, in a good way. She can't live without me. I'd say the feeling is mutual. We're meant to be together."

Erin smiled at her brother, thrilled for them. "Good. I'm so glad for the both of you."

"What about you and this Bryce guy? How's that working out?"

"I went with him on a ride-along today. He's good at his job. Do you remember the wolf I had to rescue from the zoo?"

"The shifter? Yeah."

"He's Bryce's partner."

James laughed.

"Anyway, we're going out to dinner so I need to get changed."

"If you have any troubles with him, you let me know. All right?"

"You just mind your manners with Jane."

James finished packing his last bag and saluted Erin. "Will do."

"I'll help you with your bags." She started to carry a couple of them out to his car. Living with her brother had been entertaining while she hadn't been dating anyone. They both had been off on missions so much that they weren't home at the same time all that often, stumbling over each other. But when they were together, they enjoyed playing games, going for jaguar runs, or swimming in the pool, and watching movies. Now that she was dating again, and it appeared things might get serious, she was glad she was going to have some space. She could just imagine her brother coming home and finding her kissing Bryce on the couch, or...something else.

Bryce loaded the rest of his bags in the car. "You know, we're doing this as much for you as for us."

"Oh, what's that?"

James smiled. "Hey, I haven't seen you this interested in a guy ever, and he appears to feel the same way about you. Bethany said you spent all yesterday with him and had dinner and a run with him last night. Then here you're off with him at work even, then dinner again tonight? That doesn't happen unless you're really interested. Both of you. What's happening tomorrow?"

"He's working, as if you have a need to know. I'm going out shopping with Bethany."

"And tomorrow night?"

"Not planned. *Yet.* Give Jane a hug for me and tell her I said thanks."

"She's just as glad for Bryce." James gave Erin a hug, then waved at Bryce as he pulled into the driveway.

"I'm getting changed." Erin smiled and waved at Bryce, figuring he and James would talk for a moment while she went inside to put on something else.

She was trying to figure out what to wear when she heard the door to the kitchen from the garage open and shut.

"Just me," Bryce called out. "How does a steak restaurant sound?"

"Yummy." She decided she was dressing up a little more if they were going to a steak house. She put on high-heeled boots and a long-sleeved black dress.

"Looking good," Bryce said as she came out of the bedroom.

"You look pretty good yourself." She eyed his black trousers and blue shirt, dressy, but casual.

"Your brother told me to watch myself. That you probably know as many or more martial arts moves than I do."

She laughed. "I probably do. But I'm sure I'll only have to use them against the bad guys, if any show up when we're together. Are you ready to go?"

"Yeah, I sure am."

"I hope they're happy together."

"It looks like James has moved out for good."

"They're getting married in January. The house is really mine, but when they broke up last year, he moved in with me."

Bryce got the car door for Erin. "That means we don't have to sneak around."

She laughed. "I was thinking the same thing."

After a lovely dinner and talking about everything under the sun from childhood stuff to jobs they'd worked, they headed back to her place.

"Do you want to come in for a nightcap?" She never did this with guys she'd just met. But with Bryce, she didn't want to give him up for the night. She suspected he wouldn't be averse to staying the night either, but she didn't want him to think she did this all the time.

"Yeah, sure." He sounded eager and she smiled at his enthusiasm.

"Margaritas?"

"Yeah, that sounds great."

She made them margaritas and then they sat in the living room. But it soon led to kissing. He was a consummate kisser, which made her wonder just how *many* women he'd kissed. She gave into the pleasure carrying her up and away. She wasn't used to having a relationship with a guy, but this was sure a great start.

His hands moved over the bodice of her dress to feel her breasts and she felt lightheaded, wet, eager to do something about the slow ache that was unfurling between her legs. They were kissing, his tongue licking her lips, caressing her tongue, the tequila and margarita mix making him tasty and tangy.

She began unbuttoning his shirt. She wasn't giving him up tonight. Not for anything. Then she tugged his shirt out of his trousers. They hadn't stopped kissing the whole time either, and he wasn't putting a halt to her stripping him out of his clothes. Not that she'd expected him to since they were both single and big cats and it appeared that he was just as willing to take this further. She ran her hands over his chest, caressing his nipples, and felt them pebble at her fingertips, bringing a crooked smile to his lips.

Their pheromones were taking off, indicating they were uber-interested in each other, signaling the mating call between two big cats.

He ran his hand underneath the skirt of her dress, drawing his hand higher up her thigh. Slipping his hand beneath her panties, he cupped her naked buttock.

"Bedroom," she managed to get out.

He snagged her hand and left the couch, leading them. Even though he didn't know the layout of her home, he could smell that her scent had traveled in this direction, more so than in the other, which was where the other guest bedrooms were located and where her brother had stayed.

As soon as they reached her blue and white bedroom, she slid his shirt off his shoulders and tossed it on the chest at the foot of her bed where she usually piled her clothes before she put them away or washed them. Even now, her clothes that she'd worn on the ride-along were piled up there because she'd been in a hurry to get dressed for dinner.

Bryce pulled her dress up over her head and put it on top of the other clothes on the chest. Then he pulled her close, his arms wrapped around her back, pressing her against him, kissing her again. She rubbed herself against his cock, pushing him to commit to this sooner than later.

Groaning a little, he cast her an elusive smile. She unfastened his belt and trousers, then unzipped his zipper. Her shoved off his shoes and sat her on the bed so he could pull off her boots. "Wicked."

They were too. They would be perfect in a fight, if she'd need to stab someone with a heel. He was already pulling off his socks and trousers, and then removing her stockings, leaving her bra and panties for the last.

He began to run his hands over her black satin bra, then molded his fingers to her breasts. She liked the way he touched her, and that he wasn't just getting onto the business of having sex, but spending the time to get to know her, to see what she liked, to watch her response to his touch. Her nipples stretched out to more of his touching her. But he slipped his hands around to her back and unfastened her bra, not in any rush, just making her anticipate his next move and next and next after that.

Then he removed her bra and tossed it to the stack of clothes. He slid his hand around her waist as if to keep her from falling back and bent his head to kiss her breast. His hot, wet mouth suckled her breast and her blood was on fire, her short, curly hairs drenched in anticipation. She jerked her panties off, and then tugged his boxer briefs down his narrow hips and he quickly kicked them off.

He scooped her up so she'd wrap her legs around him, and then he carried her onto the bed. Her legs wrapped around his hips, she was open to him and he could have just slid his steel-hard cock into her. But he angled himself so he could start stroking her. His finger entered her and then stroked her. She felt so wrapped up in him, she couldn't think of anything else but the way he was touching her, the stirrings of a climax, her body clenching around him.

"Ohmigod." The climax hit her, filling her with rapture, the inner muscles contracting, and she loved the way he'd brought her to orgasm.

"Hold that thought. Be right back."

"I'm on birth control, if that's—"

He smiled. "That works." Then he slid his cock inside her tight sheath.

She wrapped her legs around his hips, her hands on his waist, stroking his heated skin. He pumped into her, thrusting, and she rocked against him, loving this time with him, hoping it was just the first.

He kissed her mouth, and nuzzled her cheek, then sped up his thrusts. She could feel the tension in him rising just before he groaned with release and settled on top of her. "*You*...are amazing."

She chuckled and she wrapped her arms around him, not willing to let him go. "Can you stay the night? And get up early enough to go home and get ready for work?"

"Hell, yeah."

She smiled and he moved off her, then pulled her against him, spooning her, wrapping his arms around her. She didn't remember a time when a guy made her feel like this is just where she belonged. With him. Permanently.

"Night, Bryce."

"Night, Erin. This has been a really special day and night."

"If you want to make it really special? Just wake me when you're ready."

He chuckled. "Yeah, but if you would rather sleep, don't hesitate to tell me."

But she didn't. Not when he woke her with a kiss to her ears, neck, and throat, and she was ready.

CHAPTER 6

The next day, Erin and Bethany had just eaten grilled cheese sandwiches and lobster bisque while out shopping when she got a call from Jack. Immediately, Erin worried that something bad had happened to Bryce on the job. "Yes, Jack?"

"Hey, Bryce wanted me to let you know that on a routine drive through the city, we were hit by a drunk driver. I had to take Bryce to the hospital and x-rays revealed he has a broken leg. His phone was smashed in the wreck, or he would have given you a call. He's at the hospital now while they're casting his leg. He wanted me to tell you, just in case you couldn't get together for dinner."

"Oh, how awful." Erin had broken her leg once in the jungle, not the best place to be with an injury like that. Bryce shouldn't have that much trouble with his leg, since he could get the best of care here. "Compound or simple fracture?"

Bethany's eyes grew wide while she asked the server for the bill at the soup and sandwich shop and took care of it.

"Simple. He was lucky it didn't break the skin."

Erin was glad for that. "Oh good. Which hospital is Bryce at?"

Jack told Erin and said he had to get back to work and fill out paperwork, but he was checking on Bryce later.

"Thanks so much, Jack. I'll run in and see him and talk to you later."

"Okay, good show."

They ended the call.

"I'll take you to the hospital," Bethany said as they headed out of the restaurant. "If he's got his car at the police station, I can take the two of you there to pick it up. He'll probably need you to drive him home. You might even need to take him to your home so you can look after him." She smiled. "You gotta look at the bright side of things."

Erin let out her breath. "At least we heal faster than humans. Even so, he's got to be irritated about the whole situation."

"I betcha he'll feel much better about it when he sees you're going to take care of him."

"He might just want to be left alone." Erin climbed into the passenger's seat. "Remember how I was."

Bethany got into the driver's seat and they headed for the hospital. "Yeah, and you know how James and I wouldn't let you brood about it. We had tons of fun playing board games, cards, and watching movies. We brought you right out of that blue funk. No problem at all."

"I hope this doesn't delay his leaving the police force and joining our organization."

"It shouldn't. Training at the JAG branch will have to be delayed until he heals sufficiently, but I'm sure Martin will just give him desk duty to begin with, so he learns as much as he can about the organization and who all works there," Bethany said. "Do you have anything to fix for dinner? I could run by the grocery store and drop off whatever you need a little later."

"No, thanks, Bethany, I've got plenty of food. Especially now that James has moved out."

"I heard that he and Jane are getting married. So another hot cat bites the dust. At least Bryce will give you some company for a bit."

"*If* Bryce wants to come over. You know we're not a 'couple' yet." Still, it was stuff like this that really made them see how a prospective partner could handle being mated to the other. If they were just dating and no problems at all, they couldn't really see how the other could handle issues. Not that she wanted either of them to be injured, just to prove they were compatible. And she reminded herself they'd already done well as a team on a couple of unscheduled missions. But this was different.

Bethany only smiled.

Erin couldn't believe how anxious she was to see Bryce, hoping he wasn't in a lot of pain. *She* had been when she'd broken her leg on the mission, but that was because her brother had to create a makeshift splint for her, carry her back to their tent, gather their belongings, and carry her and their stuff out of the jungle. It took forever to make it back to their vehicle and get aid for her after that.

Bethany parked at the hospital and patted her hand. "He'll be okay. And the two of you will have a great time getting to know each other better."

Erin sure hoped so. She hadn't really dated a jaguar seriously in a couple of years and she hoped this was just the beginning with Bryce.

They soon found Bryce getting ready to make a call at the hospital. When he saw them, his glum expression changed to a big smile. "I didn't expect you to drop whatever you were doing to come here and see me."

Erin was glad they'd come for him. "Of course we did. How are you feeling?"

"Annoyed, but much better now that you are here. I've been released so that I can leave. I was just going to call Jack to come and get me."

"We've got this," Bethany said. "You know, JAG agents are always there to rescue our fellow kind."

Bryce smiled. "You can't know how good it feels to see the both of you. I hate being stuck someplace and having to wait for someone to come to my rescue."

Bethany grabbed his crutches while he settled into a wheelchair.

Erin shook her head and wheeled him to the elevator. "How does your *leg* feel?" That's what she had been really asking about. She knew from his expression he was thrilled to see them.

"It'll be healed in half the time a human's leg would heal. I was just grateful it wasn't a compound fracture."

Erin noted he had ignored her question about how his leg was feeling. He'd winced a few times and she suspected it was hurting.

"We're glad for you too," Bethany said.

They reached the bottom floor and Erin wheeled him to the doors.

Bethany motioned to the parking lot. "I'll get the car. Be right back."

"Thanks, Bethany," Erin said.

Bryce cleared his throat. "So about dinner..."

"Your house or mine? You'd probably like eating at one of our places better than running around on crutches for the time being."

"Yeah, sorry about all this."

"Are you kidding? It wasn't your fault."

Bethany pulled up and parked her vehicle at the entrance. Erin wheeled him to the passenger's door.

"Is your car at work? We can drop by the station and pick up your car. I'll take you home then." Erin helped him into Bethany's car.

"Yeah, that would be great. Thanks."

After Erin was in the back seat and Bethany in the driver's seat, Bethany drove them to the police station.

"What were the two of you doing before I ruined your plans today?" Bryce asked.

"Shopping," Bethany said, "but you know, as fellow jaguars, we're always there to help out. And we weren't looking for anything in particular. We had lunch out, so it was fine."

"I'm glad for that. About our dinner date, Erin," Bryce said, sounding as if he was a burden, no matter how much they tried to tell him he wasn't.

"I'm always flexible," Erin said. "We can either stay at your place, I'll fix a meal, or order take-out delivery. Or I can drive you to my place and you can recuperate there. How long do you get off from work?"

"Three days and then I'm stuck on desk duty for my last week on the force. This will put me behind on training for the JAG branch once I start working there. Hell, what will everyone even think?"

"That you got hit by a drunk, who, I hope, is sitting in jail now as we speak," Erin said.

"You don't mind me staying at your place? It probably would be more comfortable for you, than you staying at mine," Bryce said.

"I don't mind at all. I have lots of food still left in my fridge from James staying with me, if we want to eat what I already have."

"I think a guardian jaguar was watching over him," Bethany said.

Bryce laughed. "I have to agree with Bethany there."

Erin smiled at him. "We can do some movie or TV series marathons."

Bryce smiled.

"Yeah, Erin and I can go shopping any old time."

"You don't have to babysit me the whole time. You can just take off whenever you need to," Bryce said to Erin.

"Sure. I can do that."

"If you need anything, just call me." Bethany pulled into the parking area where Bryce's car was parked.

"I will," Erin said. Then she took Bryce's car keys and got his door for him. She noticed a bunch of his fellow officers were coming out of the police station. It must have been shift change. They were giving him thumbs-up as if he had hit the jackpot with her.

Smiling, Bethany held onto his crutches, while Erin gave him a hand to help him out of the car as he tried to avoid stepping on his broken leg. He smiled up at her as he took ahold of her hand and she was glad he wasn't so macho in front of the other guys or her that he wouldn't accept her assistance.

Bethany handed him the crutches and using them for support, he said, "Thanks, ladies."

"No problem at all," Bethany said. "I'll call you later, Erin."

"Okay. Thanks."

Other officers exited the building and were smiling at them as if they were impressed that a couple of female friends were taking care of Bryce in his hour of need.

Erin helped Bryce climb into the passenger's side of his vehicle, while Bethany waited to see if they needed her assistance. Once he was situated in the car, Erin smiled at Bethany. "Thanks again."

"Hey, it's the least I can do. Have a great time."

Jack hurried to speak to them before they left. "I thought they were keeping you at the hospital longer. I was going to drop by with something for you to eat. Is Erin looking after you?"

"Yeah. I'm off work anyway," she said.

"Okay, well, if you need anything, you just holler." Jack good-naturedly slapped Bryce on the shoulder. "But I'm sure you'll be in the best of care." He winked at Erin and waved at Bethany as she drove off.

Erin climbed into the driver's seat and readjusted it for her shorter legs, then readjusted the mirrors. "Sorry. You'll have to change it all back when you drive it again."

"No problem. I appreciate everything you're doing for me. Are you sure this is no trouble for you? I can really manage on my own."

"Not unless you want to be alone, if you're not feeling up to it, and I'd totally understand." She drove out of the police parking lot and headed for his home. "You have to eat dinner tonight anyway, and it's a real pain to get around on crutches until you get the hang of it. Besides, I'm used to my brother being around, so I'll enjoy the company now that he's moved out again."

Bryce groaned. "I don't want you to think of me as if I was just your brother."

She laughed. "Hardly. It will be nice having dinner and watching a movie tonight. You don't mind going to my place?"

"Not at all. I suspect I'm not going to be really running around much, so you might as well be more comfortable at *your* home."

She thought so too, but he was the one who had suffered an injury, so it would have been fine either way with her.

They finally arrived at his house and she helped him out of the car in the garage. And then she packed a bag for him.

"I've got a roast in the freezer if you want to have it tomorrow night," he offered.

"Sure, I'll get it." She carried his bag into the kitchen, then pulled out the roast and put it in a grocery sack he was recycling.

She noticed his display of swords on the living room wall, including the one he used on the robber at the bank.

"I used the other swords in martial arts competitions. The one I wore with my costume is strictly for musketeer, pirate, and Highland warrior garb, though it's as real as the others."

"And, most importantly, it's great to use in disarming armed gunmen involved in bank robberies."

"Yeah, that was totally unexpected."

"You need to teach me how to use a sword too. I have a buccaneer costume and it would be fun to know how to use one."

He smiled. "I can do that."

"If you have a Highland warrior costume, that must mean you have a kilt and all."

"Yep, I sure do. MacBride was my mother's maiden name. I've worn it for Halloween, but also to attend the Highland games."

"Now *that* I've got to see. Uhm, not just the kilt, but you wearing it."

He laughed.

They left his place and headed over to her house after that.

Once they settled at the house, she set him up on the couch to watch a movie. "I'll make spaghetti later, if that appeals."

"Yeah, that sounds good."

She propped his legs up on a cushion on the coffee table to elevate his broken leg. She hoped that would help reduce any swelling, and then she covered him with a soft jaguar print blanket. She handed him the TV controller. "James and I never fight over it. We both like the same shows. But you're the guest, so you decide what you want to watch. I'll get you some water. Do you need any pain medication?"

"Just the over-the-counter kind."

"Okay. I'll be right back." She figured he'd want to stay in the guest room where he could stretch out and be more comfortable, as comfortable as he could be with a newly broken leg. But that would be his choice too. His own room or hers. Preferably...*hers.*

***

Bryce thought the world of Erin for offering to do this for him when they barely knew each other, which indicated their dating was moving full-speed ahead, no matter the obstacles. He appreciated Bethany for helping them get to this point too. Even though he was in pain and normally would have preferred to be alone and just rest up, being with Erin meant all the difference in the world. He just hoped she was being honest with him and didn't mind taking care of him for tonight. He didn't expect her to have to babysit him for the rest of the week.

When the drunken perp hit Bryce's patrol car, not stopping for a red light and after Bryce had pulled fully into the intersection and the resulting accident had caused the break in his leg, he'd been angry. But seeing the setup he had now with a very willing she-cat to take care of him and for them to get to know each other better, he was thanking his lucky stars.

"It kills me not to help out a bit."

Erin smiled as she brought him the water and medicine. "Believe me, I know exactly how you feel."

"You had a broken leg before too?"

"Yeah." She sat down on the couch and he turned on the TV. "Same leg as yours, doing work, like you. Except we were out in the Amazon jungle."

"Hell, that's not the same as me at all. An ambulance took me right away to the hospital, and Jack arrested the perp. If you were in the Amazon when it happened, I imagine it wasn't any picnic."

"That part's true. James was with me on a mission. We were after a group of jaguar traffickers. We hadn't expected to find their camp so all of a sudden. They fired on us and James managed to jump to the left out of the range of a barrage of bullets. I jumped to the right, both of us firing at the gunmen. I was so near the edge of a thirty-foot ravine, I was in peril of falling. It was raining heavily, and the path was slick. I tried to scramble out of harm's way, but the rounds the traffickers were firing didn't let up. I slipped a couple of times before I fell. I managed to break my fall before I had tumbled maybe twenty feet, but I'd broken my leg in the process. I felt terrible because I put James in danger too, but he teased me that it was the greatest move I could have made. He was able to take out the guys trying to see where I had fallen.

"Once he made sure they were all dead, he had to rescue me. Believe me, that wasn't easy for either of us. What a nightmare."

"You called Martin for help?"

"Yeah, but we didn't have anyone in the area. We had to get out of there before anyone found all the dead bodies and began asking questions. Though we're a police force that has good relations with some local police forces, we didn't in that part of the world. We did call Martin on the satellite phone and he had our coordinates for getting us out of there, if we couldn't reach the airstrip on our own. But it would have taken too much time."

"I feel embarrassed to have you look after me when you went through a real ordeal."

"Don't be. After I got back home, this is exactly how I felt. James and I were both off-duty for a couple of weeks. I was off for three until the bone would heal. I hated feeling like I needed to have someone assist me with everything, even just to get a cup of tea. I'm happy to help out. Don't feel like you have to be on your best behavior either. If you want to be grouchy, or cry, or anything, feel free."

He laughed. "Believe me, if I fall and pain shoots up my injured leg, I'll be saying some choice words. Tears might even spring up in my eyes."

She chuckled and moved closer to him, their fingers interlaced on his lap. "I'm sorry you had to go through this, but I'm glad we're still going to have dinner together and more."

He arched a brow, smiling a little.

She laughed. "Movies? Breakfast, lunch, and dinners for the next couple of days?" She shook her head. "You are such a jaguar."

He only smiled and picked out a vigilante series they both were interested in and they began to watch it. He decided nothing could be better than this while his leg was healing.

After they watched several episodes, wishing they had the technology these guys were supposed to have to take down the bad guys, Erin lifted her head from Bryce's shoulder and told him she was going to make spaghetti for dinner.

"You can keep watching the show. I can see it while I'm cooking."

But he knew her back would be turned to the TV for the most part, and he also wanted to keep her company.

As soon as she started making spaghetti sauce and cooking the noodles, he stood up from the couch and grabbed his crutches. She turned to watch him.

"You know you don't have to keep me company." She stirred the noodles in the boiling water.

"I want to." He sat up at the kitchen counter.

"Can you have some wine? Uh, maybe not since you're taking pain medication."

"Yeah, probably not a good idea."

"Do you mind if I have some wine?"

"Not at all."

"Okay, I'll get you some more water." She poured a glass of cabernet for herself, water for him, and then served up the spaghetti. "This wasn't all a setup so you could see more of me during my time off, was it?"

She finished making the salad, then pulled the garlic toast out of the oven.

He chuckled. "Yeah, definitely. The perfect way to get some extra free time off from work so I could spend it all with you. Dinner in the evenings wasn't enough. Man, am I going to be ribbed about this all next week at work. I had hoped we'd arrive at the station to pick up my car before the shift change."

"You loved it."

Bryce smiled. Yeah, he did. The looks on his fellow officers' faces was precious. "They were wondering why I'd give up my job. Now they know why."

She smiled. "Did you want to watch some more of our show while we eat dinner? I'm so used to watching something when I eat when I'm alone, but when James is here, since we're family, we do it together. I'm thinking we should sit at the dining room table because of all the food we have, or I could set you up with a tray so you can prop up your leg."

"Dining room table is fine. Less trouble. That's usually what I do too. Just watch something while I'm eating."

She served up the salad and garlic bread. "How are you feeling?"

"Like maybe I should take some more pain medication."

"I kind of wondered. I'll get it for you." She went into the kitchen and got him some more medicine and returned to the table to hand them to him.

"Thanks, Erin. The spaghetti is great."

"My specialty."

***

Erin got the TV controller and started their show again, hoping that it would take Bryce's mind off his pain. Even though they healed up faster than humans, the pain was probably the same as humans felt.

They were nearly finished with their meal when Erin got a call from her boss and she wondered what was up now. She hoped he wasn't going to give her a mission when she had a very important mission herself—take care of Bryce. And she was enjoying it very much.

"Bethany told me Bryce was injured on the job today and you're taking care of him."

"Yes, sir."

"Okay, well normally I'd start him on training first thing as soon as he started to work for us in another week and a half but he'll need some physical therapy and he'll have desk duty for at least a week. If he wants to wait a week beyond that to start working for me instead, he can do that. We'll just have to play it by ear."

"All right. Thanks. I'll tell him."

"One other thing. Just to let you know, the family that you helped save Halloween night, the homeowner, Mr. Finch, wasn't exactly being honest with us. The robbers weren't run-of-the-mill robbers."

"With the firepower the robbers had, I didn't think so. What was Finch involved in?"

"He stole funds from a firm he was working for as their accountant. They're a shell corporation laundering drug money, and he was skimming off the top. We've incarcerated him in our jaguar prison and the family has been put in a safe house. That's why those men were looking for the safe. We questioned Finch for hours before he finally broke. Anyway, the money he stole from the shell corporation will be used to help pay for his incarceration. In the meantime, we had to also stage his and his family's death and make it look like the guys who came for the money, and ultimately killed the family, took off with the money and disappeared."

"Which they did once our people made their bodies disappear."

"Correct."

She couldn't believe that what seemed like just a nice family man could be a thief, working for an illegal corporation. "Is it all right to tell Bryce?"

"Yeah. I've told the rest of the team who went in to take down the robbers. Have a nice time off. Talk later."

"Thanks, boss." She set her phone down on the dining table and told Bryce what Martin had said.

"I'm glad the family wasn't injured for Finch's wrongdoings. As to the JAG branch and work, do you know any physical therapy exercises I can do?"

She smiled at Bryce. "You need to heal first."

After they ate dinner, Erin cleaned up everything.

"You know it kills me to not be able to help clean up or set the table or do anything. For a date, it doesn't give me any brownie points at all."

She shook her head. "You can't manage anything to be of any help. You just broke your leg, for heaven's sake. As far as dates go, it's been really nice—you're a great dinner and movie companion, what more could I ask for? Go on and sit on the couch and I'll be over there in a few minutes." Once she was done, she curled up next to him on the couch, leaning her head against his shoulder while they watched the show and she was thinking again about bedroom arrangements.

CHAPTER 7

Both Bryce and Erin were falling asleep on the couch while they were watching the vigilante series when she smiled up at him. "Hey, do you want to go to bed before we *can't* make it to bed?"

He chuckled. "Yeah, sure. I was feeling so relaxed, I didn't want to break up the party." He sounded as sleepy as she did.

"I know how you feel. Okay, it's your choice on bedrooms. The guest room on the left or master bedroom right beyond the living room."

"*Your* room, but I don't want to go there if I might bump you with my cast or groan in pain in the middle of the night and wake you."

"I'll take care of you. Come on, let's go to my room and we'll get some sleep. I'll get the medicine and water for you so you'll have it if you need some in the middle of the night."

"Thanks. I'll take some medicine before I go to sleep."

"I'll get your bag too. You can use the master bath and I'll use the other to take showers so you don't have to go so far to get to bed." Which was another reason to have him stay in her bedroom.

She set his bag on the floor next to the bed while he made his way to the bathroom. Then she put the medicine and glass of fresh water on the bedside table.

After she took her shower and dressed in pjs, she returned to her bedroom. Bryce had slipped under the covers so his casted leg would be on the outside of the bed. "I hope that my sleeping on this side of the mattress is okay."

"Perfect. I always sleep on the other side." It didn't take long for her to crawl under the covers. She wasn't sure if Bryce wanted to snuggle or not with the way he was feeling.

But at once, he took her hand and pulled her to join him. "This makes it almost the perfect night."

She chuckled. She suspected he wished they could make love and *that* would have made it the perfect night.

***

A month later, Bryce was happily working with Erin at the JAG branch, all healed up and ready to ask her to mate him. They'd had a lovely Thanksgiving with Jane, James, Bethany, and Jack, the only wolf in the group. Bryce had totally fallen for Erin and it had about killed him when Martin made him take a desk job and then training, while Erin and her brother had an assignment in Brazil. Bryce had texted her every chance he'd had, trying to keep up with her, even though there had been long periods he couldn't contact her. Martin told him to quit bugging him about sending another team down there to check it out every time Bryce couldn't get a call or text back from her. He'd tried her brother's number several times too.

"Sir," Bryce said, knocking on the door jamb for the second time that morning. "Send me. I can back them up."

Martin leaned back in his chair and folded his arms across his chest, his chin tilted down. "Okay, listen, next mission, you and Erin can be together. All the next missions, you can be together. But this time, you have to sit it out. Why don't you take off the rest of the day?"

"But..."

"That's an order, not a suggestion."

Bryce ran his hand through his hair and left the building. Man, had he screwed things up with the boss. He was always a professional in every situation he ever encountered. But when it came to worrying about Erin, he just couldn't help himself. Sure, he knew she was good at her job. He'd seen her in action already, twice. He still couldn't stop fretting about her.

He saw Bethany leaving her car in the parking lot and heading for the headquarters building. She smiled at Bryce. "Hey, so how's it going? Are you ready for your first real, field assignment?"

"I can't get ahold of Erin or James."

Bethany frowned. "That's probably because they're on the plane returning home."

Bryce's jaw dropped. "Why didn't she call me?"

"Phone's out? Not sure, but another agent, who was out there, said they boarded a plane and should be arriving—"

Bryce's phone jingled and he pulled it out of his pocket. "Erin! Where are you? At the airport? I'm coming for you."

He smiled at Bethany and raced to his car. "She's at the airport! She's come home."

Bethany laughed. "I can just imagine what the rest of the day will be like." Then she headed inside the building.

Bryce had big plans. As soon as he'd started working with the JAG branch, Erin had been sent off on the mission that had lasted two long, damn weeks. He'd been annoyed with the boss for sending her away, instead of finding her somewhere close by to work. But that was only because he wanted to see her every day and every night. He couldn't get enough of seeing her.

Then he smiled. The boss must have known she was coming in and that's why he told him to go home. To give him the rest of the day off to spend with Erin. Okay, so Martin wasn't such a bad guy after all.

When Bryce arrived at the arrivals for international flights, he thought he'd be taking James and Erin, and whoever the other agent was home, but Erin was the only one standing there with her luggage, smiling.

He parked. Before he got her luggage, he pulled her into his arms and kissed the living daylights out of her. "You are the only one for me. I totally love you. Man, did I miss you."

She laughed, hugging him tight still. "I can tell. Same here. Sorry, we were either running through the forest in our jaguar coats, or unable to use our satellite phones. But I'm here now. Jane picked up James. And the other agent went with them. The boss said you were anxious about me."

"Just a little."

"He said you wanted to be sent out there to rescue us." She loaded her carryon into the back seat of the car while Bryce put her other bags in the trunk.

"Yeah, I did."

"Lots of times."

"Sorry."

She smiled and kissed him again. "No reason to be sorry. It's wonderful to feel loved. But he warned me I wouldn't get any time off and instead, I'm stuck taking you on your first mission."

"Ahh, hell, I'm sorry, honey. I sure screwed up your time off."

"No, you didn't. Martin already knew I wanted to work with you on your first mission."

They got into the car and Bryce drove them to her home. "I had planned to ask you if you wanted to marry me. But I needed a little forewarning about your arrival home."

"This is enough for me."

"Yeah, but I wanted to do it right. I got champagne chilling for whenever you arrived home and steaks in the freezer. But I would have gotten fresh roses and a cake if I'd known when you'd actually get home."

"You know, all that matters is seeing you at the airport to pick me up. I couldn't wait to return and it was driving me crazy that I couldn't get ahold of you any sooner. We lost one of the satellite phones in a river, and mine stopped working. Finally, Warner was able to contact Bethany and the boss and tell them we were on our way. His battery died before he could call you and Jane."

"Martin knew. He sent me home, I thought for bugging him one too many times about not being able to contact you."

Erin smiled. "He said you were going to make a fine field agent and he couldn't wait to put you to the test. Especially while teaming you up with me so he could get you out of the office and make his life easier. He really is a great guy to work for. Believe me, he understood how you were feeling."

"I'm just so glad you're home. And I'm glad he wasn't getting ready to fire me."

"No way. So you want to get married?"

"Hell, yeah. No waiting unless you just have to." And then he wanted to change her mind, but he was reminded of James and Jane and he didn't want to get himself into that quagmire.

She laughed. "No. As soon as I got home, I was going to suggest us getting married if you didn't."

He took a relieved breath. She rubbed his thigh and he smiled at her.

"Whose house do we keep?" she asked.

"Yours? You have a swimming pool and I can't wait for you to show me some jungle gymnastics in the water as jaguars."

She smiled. "Okay, that's a deal. As long as you teach me how to use a sword."

"You got it."

When they arrived home, he carried her bags into the house and she looked at the wilting red roses in a vase. "You are so sweet."

"They're dying. I got fresh ones every few days, hoping you'd arrive home when they were still alive. I wanted them to be a surprise."

She chuckled and began stripping out of her clothes. "I love them, even if they are now wearing a vintage look."

He hurried to lock the front door and began taking off his clothes. "Bedroom, right? We're not going for a jaguar run first, I hope."

She smiled, taking off her panties last. "Not unless you insist on going for a run first."

"No."

"Take me to bed."

"My pleasure." He scooped his naked she-cat up in his arms and stalked toward the bedroom. "Making love to you first; anything else comes afterwards."

"I so agree." She smiled at the unmade bed.

"Sheets are clean," he quickly said. "I just didn't have time to make the bed."

She laughed. He *never* made the bed. Not unless they were making it together. But he was good about doing laundry and he had changed the sheets. He set her on the bed that smelled of vanilla and he tackled her. "I didn't want to wash the sheets, truth be told, because I wanted to sleep with the scent of you until you returned home. But I knew you'd prefer clean sheets."

"If the roles were reversed, I would have felt the same way about you. As it was, I was sleeping with James in a tent in the jungle."

"Next time, I hope it'll be me."

"Me too." She wrapped her arms around Bryce's neck.

He leaned down and kissed her breasts, licking each nipple. Then he pulled one into his mouth and sucked. And then the other. She was so ready for him to take her all the way. She ran her hands through his hair, loving the silky feel of it, and she smiled to smell her shampoo in it, and her coconut bodywash. "Hmm, you smell like me."

"I kept forgetting to pick some up when I went grocery shopping. It was just sort of funny when I had to keep using your soaps. I didn't mind. I felt like you were with me."

Then they began kissing again and he didn't want to be apart from her for this long ever again. He wanted to memorize the taste of her—wild and exotic from the Amazon, the scent of orchids and fresh rain—and to feel her softness all over again. He wanted to memorize her shallow breathing as he began to stroke her between the legs, to feel her dewy curls, to smell her pheromones that said she was ready for him. He wanted to memorize the rapid beating of her heart, the way her blood rushed through her veins, the way her lips parted, and her breath hitched as she writhed under his touch.

"Now," she cried out, pulling at his arm to join her.

He was aching with need and didn't hesitate to push his ready cock between her slick folds and began to thrust. She met his thrusts with enthusiasm and cried out before he was even ready. God how he loved her. Her climax stroked him as he slowed his thrusts and kissed her mouth, their tongues tangling. Then he began to push hard again, slipping his hand under her buttocks, thrusting deeper.

He felt the end coming and held on for as long as he could. And then he spilled his seed deep inside her. He pulled out and began stroking her again and she followed him with a climax of her own, crying out in pure bliss.

He rolled over onto his back and pulled her into his arms. "I don't want to ever let you go."

"Hmm, I want us to always be like this. Maybe next mission, you and I can share a sleeping bag. I heard a rumor, you might have your first field assignment tomorrow...with me."

He smiled, glad to hear it. "Good. In the meantime, wake me if you need any loving tonight."

"I sure will. You can trust me on that. Love you, you big old cat."

"I'm so glad you're home. I love you right back."

***

They made love again during the night, and late the next morning, Erin and Bryce finally made it to the kitchen. She called her brother, while Bryce was making them pancakes for breakfast. "Hey, James, I just mated Bryce and I wanted to be the first to tell you. We'll get married this December. Are you still going to make an honest woman of Jane in January?"

"Congratulations! And yep. If I don't go through with it, she'll kill me."

Erin laughed. "I need to call Bethany and then let the boss know so he can put Bryce and me on 'couple' missions whenever possible."

"Okay, I'll let you go, but congratulations to the both of you again."

When Erin called Bethany, she screamed with excitement. "I can't wait."

Erin laughed. "We'll have fun setting it all up."

Erin called Martin next and he told her he had a mission for her and Bryce then. So the rumor she'd heard was true and she was glad.

This would be the first field assignment for Bryce and the first couple mission for the two of them. She didn't even care that she would give up some of her official time off, just so she could be paired up with Bryce for his first job as a JAG field agent.

Martin briefed Erin about her first assignment with Bryce, telling her that she and he had to learn who was skimming profits off liquor sales at the jaguar-owned Clawed and Dangerous Kitty Cat Club and how he was doing it. But he wanted to tell her that the jaguar policing force had taken over the whole club to celebrate her and Bryce's and Jane and James's matings at a surprise party.

"Thanks, Martin. You're the greatest."

"Okay, put the call on speaker and I'll let Bryce in on the rest of the mission."

She did and told Bryce it was Martin calling about their first assignment.

Martin said, "The job is at the Clawed and Dangerous Kitty Cat Club. The manager suspects one of his three bartenders—mostly Larry White, because on the nights he works, sales are way off—is taking a portion of the sales. Mr. Callahan has a customer counter so he can determine how many guests he has each night. Unless a lot of visitors are coming to dance and not drink, Larry is somehow taking at least half of the sales."

"But the liquor and the amount of sales match?" Bryce asked.

"Yep, and that's what confuses the issue. The owner has security cameras both for watching the customers, but also aimed at observing the bartender and cash registers. The manager just can't figure out how the bartender is skimming off the money. At the owner's request, we installed two extra video cameras a couple of days ago before the club opened so that you can access the videos with your phones. Maybe you can catch him at it," Martin said.

"I would think that we have so many jaguar agents hanging out there, the bartender would be reluctant to steal," Erin said.

"We would too, but he's been doing this on every shift he's worked, and we always have some agents celebrating at the club at some time or another. It hasn't stopped him so far. The manager's been trying to determine how the bartender has been doing it without getting caught, but he just can't figure it out. The owner's been by there too, monitoring the videos and can't see how he's getting away with it either."

"Is Larry dangerous? Has he had any other brushes with the law?" Bryce asked.

"Not that we could discover. All agents always go in packing on a mission, just in case. He should be there an hour before the clubs opens. If we don't learn how he's doing it tonight, you'll be going in every night whenever it's his shift."

"Okay, so we arrest him and incarcerate him," Bryce said. "After we learn the truth."

"That's the score."

"Ready for your first assignment?" Erin asked Bryce.

"Yeah. Music, dancing, surveillance with my favorite cat? I couldn't have a better job."

Martin chuckled. "Good luck to the both of you." Then he ended the call.

"You really think we'll have time for dancing?" She poured them some fresh coffee.

"Hell, yeah. We'll wrap this puppy up in short order." Bryce served up the pancakes and set the plates on the table.

She sure hoped so because a lot of agents were waiting for the surprise celebration to begin. She was certain Martin had told them they would have the celebration for the engagements at a certain hour, no matter if they resolved the bartender's theft of liquor sales or not. She was excited about both the prospect of working her first case successfully with Bryce and sharing the news with all the jaguars on the force that she and Bryce were a mated couple.

***

Eager to prove his worth as a JAG agent, when Bryce and Erin arrived at the jaguar-owned and operated club, he wanted to accomplish this mission pronto. Quite a few of the agents he'd either seen at work or at the Halloween party were here, which proved just how brazen Larry was at stealing from the owner—in front of the jaguar policing force. Bryce didn't smell one human in the club, nor any wolf shifters. He and Erin ordered a bottle of beer and a glass of wine at a table for four and began watching their phones as if being together on a "date" wasn't as important as whatever they were doing on their phones.

"See anything suspicious?" Bryce asked Erin after a couple of hours. Here he thought they could wrap this up quickly, but he'd been watching the bartender carefully deposit the money in one cash register or another. Not one time did he see the bartender stick some of the money in his pocket.

"No. I wonder if he is aware that he's being watched by agents this time."

"A bunch of them are here, so maybe. Did the JAG just start video recording tonight or earlier?" Bryce wanted to see how another bartender was taking in the money from the night's sales.

"Not sure. I'll text the boss." A few minutes later, she said, "Martin's sending over the video from yesterday."

"Okay, got it." Bryce watched the video from yesterday for about fifteen minutes, then watched the live video of Larry's actions tonight. "I see a change in the setup. In the first video, there's one cash register. In the second, there are two."

"But the manager said that there's no discrepancy between the liquor usage and the amount of money in the registers."

Bryce snapped his fingers. "What if Larry's bringing in his own bottles of liquor?"

"Genius! Why don't you call the manager and ask him about the two cash registers?"

"I will. He did say he'd been watching him at the registers though. We'll need him to come down and confirm that extra bottles of liquor that don't belong to the club are behind the bar also." Bryce called the manager and asked him about the second register and if he could verify if some of the bottles of liquor weren't his.

"Hell, I was just watching to see if Larry was pocketing the money. I never even thought about him making drinks from his own stash of bottles. As to the register, you're right. Sometimes there's one, and sometimes two. I'll be right over."

"The manager is on his way over. Why don't you and I dance our way over to the bar?" Bryce asked.

"I'd like that, Mr. Jenkins."

"It's my pleasure, Ms. Jenkins." Bryce stood and offered his hand to Erin. She took it and the two of them snuggled close while she continued to monitor the video on her phone and he guided them through the dancers on the floor, taking a round-about way to the bar.

By the time three songs had played and he saw the manager come in the back door and glance around the club, looking for Erin and Bryce, they were nearly to the bar. Bryce waved at the manager, who stalked across the floor and the three of them headed behind the bar. Larry had his back to them, mixing a margarita while the manager looked for liquor bottles that weren't his own.

Larry turned around and saw Erin and Bryce. "You can't be back here. Leave now or I'll call the cops."

"I authorized them to be back here," the manager said, coming from the opposite direction.

Larry swung around to see the manager standing there holding a box of bottles of liquor. "Yours, I presume."

Bryce arrested the bartender and figured he and Erin would be taking him to lockup, but another agent at the club came around the bar and said he'd take the prisoner instead. The agent smiled. "Enjoy the rest of your night."

Martin suddenly showed up at the club and stopped the music. "I just want to say congratulations are in order for Bryce's first successful mission and that we have two of our JAG agent couples getting married: Jane and James and Erin and Bryce."

Everyone clapped and cheered them. Then the music played again and several couples began dancing.

"It's not just a job," Bryce told Erin as they danced nice and close again, only this time they were strictly here to enjoy themselves, but he realized just how much the agents cared about each other.

"No. We're family."

"I don't think I've seen so many agents here at one time."

"Martin reserved the club for us. But I suspect the owner did it for free to help us catch a thief."

"I think that was the easiest job I've ever been on."

Erin smiled up at him. "Maybe, but the manager and the owner couldn't figure it out. They just needed a fresh perspective. Not all our jobs involve gun play, or jaguar teeth, but I'm sure you'll get plenty of that in the years to come."

Bryce kissed her mouth. "Sorry, that you didn't get any time off."

She drew closer to Bryce on the dance floor, rubbing her body against his like a big cat wanting some loving. "This is not too shabby for working a first mission, don't you agree?"

"Not too shabby at all."

Martin stopped the music again and called out, "Hey, just got a call about a fight between two male jaguars over a female downtown. Do I have any volunteers to handle it?"

Erin kissed Bryce and hugged him close, dancing to the nonexistent music, her brother dancing slowly by with Jane and he winked at Erin.

They may be workaholics, but sometimes it was just plain time to celebrate.

EPILOGUE

It was Erin and Bryce's first anniversary of having met and time for Halloween again. It would always be a special time for them.

Erin smiled at Bryce's MacBride kilt. "Going commando?"

"Naturally, for what comes after the party." He looked over her long MacBride kilt as if he was trying to determine if she was too.

"You know it."

"I should have guessed. We usually think along the same lines when it comes to planning what follows. I thought it was cute that Bethany is going to be dressed like she's one of our kinsmen."

"Which she is."

"True enough." He opened the mail he hadn't gotten to and frowned. "Well, good news and bad. The good news is that we got the check for the sale of my house. The bad news is that it's more than the amount they allow for an online deposit."

Erin opened her mouth to speak, then shook her head. "Okay, that means dropping by the bank on Halloween and of course, wouldn't you know, today we have a super moon. Got your sword handy?"

Bryce smiled at her and slipped it on his belt. "You?"

She attached her sword to her belt, glad he'd been giving her lessons on swordsmanship for the show they were going to perform tonight at the Halloween party. Everyone was excited about it. "Ready."

Not that they were expecting a bank robbery to take place...but they were JAG agents...and prepared for anything.

"I've never felt safer going to the bank," he said, taking her hand as he led her outside to his car. "You cast a spell over me, you know, that first time."

She smiled at him as he got her car door for her. "You fought your way right into my heart." She wrapped her arms around his neck and kissed him, their kilts pressed tight against each other. "I don't know." She felt his cock stirring to life. "I might not be able to wait until after the Halloween party to see what you have for me under your kilt."

He laughed. "Let's make the bank deposit, and we can return home and I'll make another deposit before we head over to the Halloween party."

She knew he was the right one for her. No matter the trials they had to face in their line of work, they were always ready for lots of kitty cat loving.

***

Bryce hadn't believed he would have given up his opportunity to be a homicide detective with the human police force to join the jaguar policing force until he'd set his sights on one determined jaguar in training, amazed at her moves in the water, "fighting" against her opponent, a male jaguar. Bryce and Erin had taken down two jaguars in the Amazon River, just from using the same techniques in the training she'd put him through earlier this year. She wasn't just a beautiful cat, but smart, a worthy opponent, and fun to be with. But today, she was a sexy lass and all his.

One full moon a year ago had made that Halloween even more magical. And now, the super moon was on full display. He drove them to the bank and saw a car with its engine running, the driver looking anxiously around.

It might be nothing, but Bryce skipped the drive-thru and parked the car next to the running vehicle. "Ready for action?" he asked Erin.

"Always."

"Let's do it."

And in they went, ready for any eventuality. They were a JAG agent-couple team, after all, and loving every minute of it—the good and the bad—through bullet wounds and broken bones and all the loving in between.

ABOUT THE AUTHOR

Bestselling and award-winning author **Terry Spear** has written over sixty paranormal romance novels and seven medieval Highland historical romances. Her first werewolf romance, *Heart of the Wolf,* was named a 2008 *Publishers Weekly*'s Best Book of the Year, and her subsequent titles have garnered high praise and hit the *USA Today* bestseller list. A retired officer of the U.S. Army Reserves, Terry lives in Spring, Texas, where she is working on her next werewolf romance, continuing her new series about shapeshifting jaguars, writing Highland medieval romance, and having fun with her young adult novels. When she's not writing, she's photographing everything that catches her eye, making teddy bears, and playing with her Havanese puppies and grand-baby. For more information, please visit www.terryspear.com, or follow her on Twitter, @TerrySpear. She is also on Facebook at http://www.facebook.com/terry.spear. And on Wordpress at:

Terry Spear's Shifters
http://terryspear.wordpress.com/

ALSO BY TERRY SPEAR

Heart of the Cougar Series:
Cougar's Mate, Book 1
Call of the Cougar, Book 2
Taming the Wild Cougar, Book 3
Covert Cougar Christmas (Novella)
Double Cougar Trouble, Book 4
Cougar Undercover, Book 5
Cougar Magic, Book 6

* * *

Heart of the Bear Series
Loving the White Bear, Book 1
Taming the White Bear, Book 2, (TBD)

* * *

The Highlanders Series: Winning the Highlander's Heart, The Accidental Highland Hero, Highland Rake, Taming the Wild Highlander, The Highlander, Her Highland Hero, The Viking's Highland Lass, His Wild Highland Lass (novella), Vexing the Highlander (novella), My Highlander

Other historical romances: Lady Caroline & the Egotistical Earl, A Ghost of a Chance at Love

* * *

Heart of the Wolf Series: Heart of the Wolf, Destiny of the Wolf, To Tempt the Wolf, Legend of the White Wolf, Seduced by the Wolf, Wolf Fever, Heart of the Highland

Wolf, Dreaming of the Wolf, A SEAL in Wolf's Clothing, A Howl for a Highlander, A Highland Werewolf Wedding, A SEAL Wolf Christmas, Silence of the Wolf, Hero of a Highland Wolf, A Highland Wolf Christmas, A SEAL Wolf Hunting; A Silver Wolf Christmas, A SEAL Wolf in Too Deep, Alpha Wolf Need Not Apply, Billionaire in Wolf's Clothing, Between a Rock and a Hard Place, SEAL Wolf Undercover, Dreaming of a White Wolf Christmas, Flight of the White Wolf (2018), A Billionaire Wolf for Christmas (2018), SEAL Wolf Surrender (2019), Silver Town Wolf: Home for the Holidays (2019)

SEAL Wolves: To Tempt the Wolf, A SEAL in Wolf's Clothing, A SEAL Wolf Christmas, A SEAL Wolf Hunting, A SEAL Wolf in Too Deep, SEAL Wolf Undercover, SEAL Wolf Surrender (2019)

Silver Bros Wolves: Destiny of the Wolf, Wolf Fever, Dreaming of the Wolf, Silence of the Wolf, A Silver Wolf Christmas, Alpha Wolf Need Not Apply, Between a Rock and a Hard Place, All's Fair in Love and Wolf (2018), Silver Town Wolf: Home for the Holidays (2019)

White Wolves: Legend of the White Wolf, Dreaming of a White Wolf Christmas

Billionaire Wolves: Billionaire in Wolf's Clothing, A Billionaire Wolf for Christmas (2018)

Highland Wolves: Heart of the Highland Wolf, A Howl for a Highlander, A Highland Werewolf Wedding, Hero of a Highland Wolf, A Highland Wolf Christmas

* * *

Heart of the Jaguar Series: Savage Hunger, Jaguar Fever, Jaguar Hunt, Jaguar Pride, A Very Jaguar Christmas, You Had Me at Jaguar (2019)

Novella: The Witch and the Jaguar (2018)

* * *

Romantic Suspense: Deadly Fortunes, In the Dead of the Night, Relative Danger, Bound by Danger

* * *

Vampire romances: Killing the Bloodlust, Deadly Liaisons, Huntress for Hire, Forbidden Love

Vampire Novellas: Vampiric Calling, The Siren's Lure, Seducing the Huntress

* * *

Other Romance: Exchanging Grooms, Marriage, Las Vegas Style

* * *

Science Fiction Romance: Galaxy Warrior

Teen/Young Adult/Fantasy Books

The World of Fae:
The Dark Fae, Book 1
The Deadly Fae, Book 2
The Winged Fae, Book 3
The Ancient Fae, Book 4
Dragon Fae, Book 5
Hawk Fae, Book 6
Phantom Fae, Book 7
Golden Fae, Book 8
Falcon Fae, Book 9
Woodland Fae, Book 10

The World of Elf:
The Shadow Elf
Darkland Elf

Blood Moon Series:
Kiss of the Vampire
The Vampire...In My Dreams

Demon Guardian Series:
The Trouble with Demons
Demon Trouble, Too
Demon Hunter

Non-Series for Now:
Ghostly Liaisons
The Beast Within
Courtly Masquerade
Deidre's Secret

The Magic of Inherian:
The Scepter of Salvation
The Mage of Monrovia
Emerald Isle of Mists (TBA)

Made in the USA
Las Vegas, NV
13 November 2023

80717356R00069